FALL TO THE

Rising
Moon

ZACKARY GIBSON

ISBN 978-1-0980-5476-2 (paperback)
ISBN 978-1-0980-5578-3 (hardcover)
ISBN 978-1-0980-5477-9 (digital)

Christian Faith Publishing, Inc.
832 Park Avenue
Meadville, PA 16335
www.christianfaithpublishing.com

Printed in the United States of America

INTRODUCTION

This story isn't about heroes, villains, and nothing short but the grim reality that happiness never survives but that revenge is forever.

My dreams wondered, a feeling I cannot shake like fog hanging over where I lay. Darkness filled my eyes but gave way to light. I lay gazing into the clouds; the breeze filled my lungs as it washed over me like a wave; the grass formed around my body as if holding me tight like a mother holding its child. This last year rolled through my mind, but I couldn't focus on a single thought. Folks of birds soared through the air.

Damn, life must be so free up there, unconcerned with the life of humans. It must be beautiful, but soon I shielded my eyes from the glare of the sun. The wind whipped, howled as I close my eyes to find a calm place within my mind, but as soon as I do, a shadow loomed over me. I felt no fear as I knew who it was because of the scent oils that he wore. Honestly, I don't know how ladies enjoy that strong smell; it makes my nose burn.

I said, smiling, "Hello, brother, I see you're skipping out on training again. Our brother must be looking for everywhere to find his punching bag. Is that what I am now, huh?" My eyes were still closed. I had to get away for a moment.

My brother sat next to me, but he said nothing for a moment.

"Back from hunting so early this time, Jason?"

"Yes, it seems like it could get bad again."

3

I breathed deep with loathing. I dislike the rambling of schemes of old men. Yet they will come again and again. I glanced over to him as he unwrapped a white cloth around his hands though it runs halfway up his arms. He is only a year older than me at seventeen. He has long jet-black hair, clean shaved, a pretty boy—my brother calls him—for his lack of "warrior" look.

He looked toward me. With his sharp chin with long skinny thin arms and legs, you thought the man lived off grass but he is strong and quick. Not only that, but in the last year, we, and especially him, have become great warriors since father unexpectedly died.

I looked away from him and back to the birds flying.

"How you been?" Jason asked, pushing his hair out of the way to see me better.

I took a minute to answer. I sighed deeply, but it turned into a smile. "I know everyone is changing, and I'm growing tired of the games I see around me. It's trying to suck me in. It's a web, and I can't feel I can get out."

"I love our family," I said but he could tell the sadness in my words. I looked down to the green grass. "Sometimes I'd rather leave it all behind and find somewhere it's quiet."

I heard him snicker. "What kind of boy am I hearing? William, you walk away from something difficult." He paused for a moment. "Nah, you're just growing soft, little brother, since you met that girl."

My eyes lifted up and looked to the horizon; the forest deep of mystery filled my eyes.

"Plus then, you never get a shot to prove to Chris that father was wrong."

I looked up to the sky and growled and fell back into the soft earth. Father is dead with Uncle Jack.

He breathed deep. "You know it's not bad, right?" Jason pushed. "You have a much easier life than those who are not us. We got lucky unlike most in this world. I know it's easier sometimes to fight on the battlefield than talk in the shadows of politics. Worry not, brother, that's why I spend most of my time away with my men 'hunting' to lessen the burden for you."

I looked at my brother through the corner of my eye. "Ha ha," I jested. "Oh, brother, it must be so dangerous hunting deers and shadows." I laughed as I punched him in the arm.

With an unanticipated reaction, Jason leaped on me, putting me in a headlock. "Yeah, you think so? I could kill you long before you even knew I was there, runt."

I growled as I felt him squeezing harder. "Though who are you calling runt?" I choked out. "I would smell you before you had the chance."

His grip tightened. I could feel the blood rushing to my head, threatening to make me lose consciousness. I growled and dug deep, pulling forward and struggling to my knees. Jason's light frame is easy to lift with how much larger I am than him by at least seventy pounds. But in the last moment before I think I can before passing out, I used all my strength and jumped up just enough to let gravity do the rest, threw my body back toward the ground, the full weight slamming into him. I heard the air burst from his lungs, his grip loosening just enough to grab his hands and spin around while unsheathing my dagger on my belt loop and pressed it to his neck. His hands raised up in submission as he gasped for air. I slowly pressed the blade harder to his skin but not enough to cut him.

I leaned down with an evil grin. "I hope you do, brother, because if I catch you…" and I made a jester with my finger going across my throat. I held eye contact with him for a moment longer for added effect and the roar of laughter as his face tightened up. Jason smacked the blade away and rolled backward to rolling up onto his feet before standing. Both of us stared each other down.

Jason whistled and looked back to four older men who are his personal guards who are dragging a man with a sack on his head. I pointed with my dagger. "A friend of yours, brother?"

"A gift for our sisters to play with."

But before I could speak, he snapped out the name Harris.

A cloaked man walked forward with a large bow strapped to his back. Two blades now. I watched the soldier walk forward, sporting a dark green cloak, holding out two blades to my brother. Jason stabbed down one blade into soft green earth, his eyes never leaving my gaze. A smile crept over his face, and he tossed the blade a few feet short from where I was standing. The man walked away to the group of men. My eyes met my brother's as my adrenaline started to pump. I crept carefully forward, watching my brother in case of him attacking as I reached down for the blade.

As I reached down, I heard another voice come from behind me coming up the hill. I looked back just for a split second to see my oldest brother, Chris, in his heavy black cloak with bear fur on the shoulders. His beard is thick with long black patch that covers a scar over his left eye. My sisters, at his side, they are young but are equally terrifying in their own ways.

But in that moment, seeing them, Jason rushed forward, his blade cutting against the soft grass, bringing up dirt. His strike was so fast I barely have time to jump backward, barely missing the point of his blade, but the dirt that was taken up got in my eyes, my footing stumbled, and I started falling but caught myself with my other arm and spun around instinctually thrust my blade, aiming for up, almost piercing my brother's throat. His eyes are sharp as well as his instincts. He adjusted his body to barely avoid the blade and knocked the blade out of the way, stepping back.

I raised to my feet and wiped the dirt from my eyes. The group of soldiers watched silently as we studied one another. Jason ran his hand through his hair, grinning. "You're too stiff, little brother. Relax, iBook, there's no pressure," pointing his blade to those around us, stopping his point of his blade at our oldest brother—a motion few men would even think of doing. He is undoubtedly one if the greatest warriors and my tutor. Very few men even can grabble with him, let alone face him one on one with his great axe. And for being a much taller than us, both around 6.5', he is shockingly fast at a close distance.

"William!" Chris roared, "finish proving your worth that all those blows got through your thick skull."

I dug deep, my anger boiling up inside. But I focused it down at my brother. Jason grinned, leaned in, and dashed forward, leaping with each foot to close the distance. Just as he got into range, he spun his body and overarched his blade coming down full force. I should move out of the way, but I pulled my blade up and roared, putting all my strength into blunting the blow. The steel rang as they smashed together. As in that moment, everything slowed down as his body came down. I cocked back my fist and uppercut him with all my might, slamming my fist into his jaw, lifting him up off the ground. His body arched, and those watching winced as his body fell to the ground.

Jason, clearly dazed from the blow, tried to stand, but I lowered my blade toward his eyes. He stared up at me, clearly defeated. Our eyes met, but there was no anger in them but pride. I grinned and stabbed my blade into the ground. I lowered my hand, and Jason grabbed it, I help him to his feet as he grabs his sore jaw.

"I will have to return the favor one day," he said, laughing while trying to hide the pain.

I looked back. Chris was already behind, us towering over us both. He always has the look in his eye like he is always on the edge of snapping, but his face is relaxed and calm.

"Clean yourselves up. You both look like pathetic. Tonight's going to be a feast for father. Many guests will be here. So I expect your best."

"Oh, there'll be plenty ladies around tonight for you to fill with," I poked fun. My brother went to laugh, but the look from Chris made it only come out as chuff.

"Soon I expect a report."

Jason turned and bowed slightly, not entirely out of respect.

Chris looked toward me. "I will see you soon, little brother, and we will have a better contest," then he turned and walked away.

Jason nudged me. "I think that's the closest you will ever come to a compliment."

"Yeah, probably. Come, brother, the day is far from over."

My brother called his men over, and they collected their prisoner.

I saw our sisters smiling at us and walked up to me. Both are twinning. Amanda is taller than her sister. "Having fun?" my older sister said with a sly tone.

I went to speak, but Sarah cut me off. "Hmm, not as much as we will be later."

Both of their eyes stared that made me uneasy. My sisters hugged me and squeezed me tight, making the uneasy feeling pass.

"When are you going to come watch us have our fun?" They both smiled at each other in an almost innocent twisted way.

I stared at them both. "Hmm, I think I will pass. Glad Mom taught you ladies that, and from the bottom of my heart, I hate to be a kill joy."

Sarah laughed with almost a snort. "Good one."

Amanda rested her head against mine, her eyes piercing into mine. Her lips turned into a frown. "You act like you don't love us."

Then with a shiver, I felt my other sister's hand slid up my back. I looked down to my left. Sarah's eyes, big, full of something dark. "Yet is that true, brother? Have you no place anymore in your heart? You know I love you." Both were squeezing me hard till they made funny sounds, telling me to stop.

"Honestly, you both are just terrifying," I said with a smile.

Two girls' eyes looked up, eyes wide. "You really think so?" they both said together, clearly pleased by what I said.

"You both are broken I swear."

"Leave him alone, you hell spawns." The girls looked over to Jason who was walking up. "He thinks you both hideous creatures."

They gasped as if stuck by arrows. "You know that's not true, brothers," as they struck a dramatic pose that looked ridiculous.

I laughed and pushed past them both and started moving back to the city. "You three are something special."

Sarah whined and yelled, "You can't choose your family, jerk."

I turned around but kept walking forward. "You are right, but I can walk away," I said while shaking my head. The walk back the not long but part-hearing those two friends to explain the amount of fun they will have fun with the prisoner I think will give me nightmares.

I tried and focus on the fields of wheat, golden yellow for acres, and the hardworking families that work them. Soon I stood in the shadow wooden walls that were the protection to most folks, but buttering dragged into this place is a death sentence to a lot of souls lately. Each step closer, the sounds of a city filled my ears, soldiers talking to one another on the walls as the gates open to busy folks running through their daily business. A large fountain in the center with a mother statue in the center holding her child to her chest. I watched as children played around it. Folks booed and hit the man that's being dragged in; folks are getting used to seeing it more and more lately. But other than that, it's a beautiful place to be.

I closed my eyes, let it fill me in until I am lost in the moment when I heard some rushing up to me, screaming my name. I turned just in time to reach out as a beautiful woman leaped through the air and barreled into me, almost plowing me over. Her eyes are misty gray, hair brown, spikey, short, with a smile that makes you want to kiss her forever. But as I held her high feet dangling, I tried to kiss her, but as I closed my eyes, instead of feeling her soft lips, I felt her dense forehead crushing against mine at full speed. Pain shot down my spine as my eyes rolled back. I heard her roaring in laughter before choking, "What took you so long? I was waiting here all day."

My brain was barely able to focus. I grabbed her by the shirt. "What the hell, Quinn!" Towering above her, she looked up to me, her eyes piercing into mine, then she reached up and grabbed a fistful of my hair and kissed me deep. I could hear kids making different sounds of disgust and cheers. Quinn pulled away, and I could see her get tense. I looked to where she was looking and saw my sisters leaning against a couple of crates. Their gaze felt like daggers piercing through you.

"Look at this, sister," Amanda said to her sibling. "Does a cat want to lie with lions?" Their usually less aggressive personality is peeling back to reveal darker side.

I stepped in between them. "Ladies, this is not the time nor place."

Hinting at growing interest in the folks around us, Quinn went to posture against my sisters, but she noticed the reaction in my face and backed down.

Sarah sneered, "Some time, we will get to play with you, little cat," as they walked away, escorted with their person handlers. Then a voice between me and Quinn startled us both. As we saw, Jason walked between, his hair covering most of his face. "Be careful,

Quinn. Those two are not to be taken lightly. Trust me, I would know."

Quinn jabbed him in the arm, making him rub like it hurt him. "I hate it when you sneak up on me." The statement only made him grin more.

Anyway, we all started walking through the town when Quinn grabbed us both and led us into one of the alleys. "Look, you two, I need you both to keep a secret." The sound of her voice made me anxious.

"So what is it?" Jason pried.

"Look, I know you both been busy and it's hard to get around to me, but I have been changing," she said while grabbing the back of her neck. "I didn't know who to go to about by one person."

Jason eyes lock with hers. "What's going on?" I say with caution.

She tried to find the words, but instead, she pulled out and held out a necklace with a blue jewel hovering in between a small metal sphere, and in a flash, a small blue flame hovered in her hand. It's small, but me and Jason were in awe and in immediate concern. I quickly looked around to see if anyone was watching.

"Damn you, Terry," I growled.

Jason grabbed her hand, and the flame went out. "You should keep that to yourself, girl," he bit out.

"It's an amulet that channels her will through."

Me and Jason both stared at each other and looked back to her. "Honestly, Quinn, I would lose it."

Her eyes glared at him.

"If Chris were to see you with that, he would have you killed."

Her eyes dropped to the ground.

"Power attracts power, Quinn. Remember that."

"So have you used it yet? How long ago did you start seeing Terry about this?" I pressed.

Her eyes didn't back down from ours. "About a month ago."

"Why didn't you tell me?" My voice was full of concern.

Looking into her eyes, her jaw tight, she said, "I did try when you saw my hands slightly burned. It wasn't from a pot like I told you. I could hardly control it, so I set up a meeting with him, and I have been going regularly. Look, don't be mad. I just needed help."

I sighed, breathing deep. "I am not mad, Quinn. Just need to look out for you."

"I can take care of myself," she bit back.

My shoulders tightened up, but Jason butted in. "Look, it's for everyone's interest that we look out for one another. There are many interests by many people. We just don't want you to be on that list."

"I know," she sighed. "I will be safe I promise," hugging us both then turned and ran away.

Moments later, she was lost within the crowds of people.

"Do you feel it, brother?" Jason asked. "It's like a mist of something foul."

"It will be fine if we keep it that way, I guess." Then me and my brother headed off in separate paths in the winding streets. Soon the streets were filled more with soldiers than people as I made the steady climb home.

Soon the home my mother and father built comes into view. I crested the lip of the hill. Groups of soldiers crowded in a large circle as men battle one on one to test their prowess. These contests are always full contact with sharp blades. Rarely does a contest end with fatal wound, but this world is dangerous, and Chris trains the men with that in mind.

I made my way to small wall overlooking the yard and gazed into the distance. Beyond the walls the tall wheat fields stretch for acres over rolling hills until it reaches the forest and tall mountains, many different peoples live drawing my curiosity. Me and my mother would sit up here and gaze out into the world, but when our mother had passed away from giving birth to my youngest brother, Terry, things got bad. She was unlike any women you ever knew. Her family was feared and prized executioners. She could get information out of anyone. She instilled her skills into her daughters and surprising amount of care to her children. Especially Chris, father pushed him past his limits every day to make him the best. Both father and Chris are the same: strong and great leaders but lack any real emotion to help them cope with life outside of a battle. That's where my mother came. She wasn't the glue but the steel bolts that made our family unbreakable.

Then she passed; we couldn't believe it. Terry was different from the start. You could feel mother's power living through him, but his body could not handle it. His cries of pain and sickness followed his every step because of his gift of magic. Father became almost a shell of himself, obsessed with how to save his youngest son. He forgot about the rest of us, and Chris took it the worst, becoming ruthlessly aggressive to others, and his hatred grew for Terry and his father.

The girls did the only thing they knew and modeled themselves after mother, but they have become, deep down, far more twisted—and lastly, me. When I am not in the embrace of death or Quinn, I try to escape it all. Terry stays locked away, but when it's time to eat, even then it's rare.

"My lord," a man called out to me, breaking me from my deep thought. I turned to see three men close to my age wearing black cloaks. "Your brother requests your presence."

I smiled as I lean against the rail. "Which one?"

"Terry, my lord."

That man always seems to know things before they happen. "Okay then, thank you, men."

The three lightly bowed and headed away. I looked back to the sun setting. *Here we go,* I thought to myself. I walked down that ramp and through the courtyard, and two soldiers opened the large wooden doors. Music filled my ears to large hall with an overhanging balcony that overlooked the hall.

Sergeant of the guard walked up to me, holding out a huge dark mead.

"Gustav, not now." But when I pushed past, he blocked my path. His armor covered most of his body. His hair is balding but a man not to be taken lately.

"Trust me, William, you're going to want to go down those stairs not sober."

"Why?" I asked, slightly impatient.

"Your sisters dragged that poor fellow down there, and if you're going to see your brother, you will have to go by that room."

I sighed. "Right, like always, my main man," and took the mug and drank deep.

"That's right. Drink deep. I have been around long enough to know it's not worth going down there sober."

I wiped my face clean and handed the man back his mug. My body is not quite suited for drinking, but I can handle my own.

Gustav laughed. "See, men," calling to soldiers at a large table, "I will make a proper man out of him yet." And he roared with laughter and walked away.

I looked up before walking to see my brother looking down on me, his eyes studying mine. But I didn't wait long and headed down a flight of stone stairs. Unlike the rest of the house, this is newly built by my sisters so they can enjoy their craft in private. But even more so, when my brother's fits happen, our home doesn't burn down. Each step down, the underlit hall's screams start to echo. Coolness of the halls and periodic screams followed by laughter kept me on edge as I walked slowly. Soon I came up to a door on my right that swings open, causing me to freeze as my sister walked into view. In the darkness, her skin looked pale, her black hair sided over her shoulders, her tight black dress gripped the curves of her body. She would be to die for if it wasn't for the blood that covers her hands that turns a man's blood cold. She breathed deep as her hand rose, bringing up a glass up to her lips with a dark liquid that I am questioning if it's wine or not. Her head slowly turned, and her eyes met mine. "Hello, brother."

"Hey, sis. Having fun?" I said with not enough confidence as I approached her.

"Why so cautious? We are family, you know," but the words seem to lack meaning.

I walked until I stood before her. I reminded myself I am happy to have it that way. Another scream of agony rang from the room when my other sister yelled for her. I looked down my sister with more liquid courage. "I think you're missing out on the fun."

"Ha, he will break far too soon for my liking." Then in a blur her back is leaning against me with her eyes looking up to mine. "You should have seen mother." There was a hint of sadness in her voice. She was unlike anything I could hope to achieve.

"Well I think it's a first that a statement like that could actually make feel sad for you as a man who is experiencing the end of his life."

She breathed her hot breath, filling the air around me. "The world is a cruel bitch, I suppose." And she raised the glass for another drink.

But before I could speak, the door opened, just enough for my sister's twisted grin to be seen and her hand to grab Amanda's and drag her back. In a flash, the door slammed in my face. I looked down to see my hand slightly trembling, then I turned to see the other door ahead of me, a red glow illuminating from underneath. *I didn't drink enough,* I thought to myself. Then I heard a voice. Through the door, I couldn't make out a word, then it went quiet.

"William, come in. Everything is fine," he said with a shaky voice.

I grabbed the handle, and I opened the door to see my brother sitting on a table overlooking a fireplace. His hair was turning even more gray over these last few years. His body is thin but is actually looking better than he has recently. If it was for his condition, he would probably be a hit with the ladies.

"Come in. Stop staring. You're going to make me feel like you're going to catch something."

"Sorry." I shook my head. "I had too much to drink."

"Ah, is Gustav testing you again?"

"No." I looked back down the hall.

"Ah yes, it's not the most pleasant of roommates to hear that from time to time. How did you know I was wanting to see you, brother?" Terry pushed up his glasses.

"I have my ways, but for what you really wanted to talk about is Quinn."

"Yes."

I looked at him sharply, my body growing tense. His hands raised up with his palms open. "Calm down. She came to me. It was only a matter of time. She is like me."

"No, she isn't," I bit out.

"Look, you are out of your depth. She is going to hurt herself or others if I don't help her. You are going to get her killed by dragging her into this life. It's too late," he said low.

The statement made me walk closer, flexing my size over him.

"I have her one of my talismans to help her focus and at least, she won't be able to channel enough through it to hurt herself."

I growled but I know he is right.

He walked closer to me, put hand on my shoulder. "Brother, it will be all right, especially to you since you treat me more fair than the others."

"And what of the girls?" I said questioningly.

He laughed. "I live down the hall way from that." Pointing down the hall, he said, "Do you trust them completely?" half smiling.

I laughed lightly just in case they somehow hear me. "That's a pretty good point."

"Now let me rest, brother. I am not as fiery as the rest of you. I need my rest. Night, brother. I hope you feel better."

Time slipped away as I made my way back out through gloomy halls that were now quiet and through the main hall where the night was full of normal rough housing. I walked outside. It's late. The moon shone its light high in the sky, storms clouds gathering in the distance. Chris, my oldest brother, stood watching two soldiers fight. His eyes always watching each movement, somehow studying each swing and counter to far more detail turn I could.

"Where is Jason?" I asked him.

"Where do you think?" his voice low, like chasing some poor lady's skirt. "How did your meeting with the creature go?" His voice sounded cold.

"I found out what I wanted."

"Good," he said quickly. "Hold," he growled to the two young men. "Go get food and drink. Leave me with my slacker of a brother." I felt the tension in the air between us grow thick. I looked to my brother, but I saw my sisters walked out the front and walked past us, heading into the town, almost like nothing even happened. My eyes drifted away. "Can you even concentrate?" he snapped at me.

I sneered and faced him again. "Give me a few more years, and I will be able to take you one with no problem," I boasted, sticking out my chest and kneeling down, grabbing a blade from the ground.

"Oh, I see. Let's see what you learned so far," grabbing a wooden practice axe.

"Really, you would disgrace me," I roared.

Then he smiled, which is rare. "It's what you deserve."

The sight made my rage boil over as I charged on him quickly, swinging sword at him. He laughed and blocked it to the side and threw me to the ground. I lunged from one knee to strike low, hoping to catch him off balance. He noticed my attack quickly and roared and lifted his leg out of the way, just in time to dodge my thrust, and he pushed to the side. His other leg swung straight into my ribs, knocking the breath out of me. I rolled a few feet and came to a stop, grasping my ribs as I coughed. I went to get back on my feet when I felt his wooden axe scraping against my neck.

"You're dead, little brother," he was saying in a low voice. "You best hope you can make it a few more years." He laughed and reached his hand down to me to help me up. I sneered and smacked it away and lifted myself up. I had to look up at the giant warrior chief towering over me.

He smiled. "Glade too see your ability to use my own strength to pick myself up after that."

"I have taken down men in battle, brother. Don't make light of me," I growled.

"But not a real warrior, my brother," he roared, his body tensing.

I heard the front door open up and a slim man walked out, and to my surprise, I see Terry, my youngest brother, walking out of the house. He looked worried.

"What could possibly bring you up out of your tomb?" he asked in a serious tone. "What's the problem?"

"Something feels wrong out there," he said in a cautious tone. "Something is coming. I can feel it in my bones. "If I take advice from you…" Terry looked at him with uncertainty and looked to the moon as if it held all the secrets.

"Maybe we should send a few more guards out to get the girls," I stammered out. A chilly feeling crept up my spine.

Chris looked at us both, but even through his bravado, he nodded and beckoned two guards that were close to the house. The guards jogged over to their chief. Chris looked down at them. "Get the girls back now, just in case. Put more guards on the wall." Chris looked over to me. "Get some sleep, little brother, you're exhausted. I need you rested just in case."

I went to talk back to him, but his glare at me was the final judgment. I turned and walked toward the house. I looked out into the woods looming in the distance. The darkness from the woods crept in as if it's alive. If we only truly understood what was coming, we could have been better prepared. But it was already too late.

CHAPTER 1

Blood Moon Rises

I went to bed shortly after my training with my brother. I was exhausted and covered in bruises. My body felt so heavy. Sleep overcame me easily. But my dreams were tormenting me tonight. I kept tossing and turning, trying flashes of blades clashing together, sending sparks, illuminating the void around me, and each time, a large shadow would creep closer and closer, reaching out to me, but as its cold black hands went to grip my throat, I heard a loud bang and screams coming from outside of my window.

I sat up with a jolt, my body covered in a cool sweat. My heart felt like it was beating against my chest. I heard a commotion in the main hall. I jumped out of bed and opened my door when I heard some kind of ghastly howl. I rushed down the stairs to see my brother Chris with his massive axe slumped against the wall. Two bodies lay before him that had axe wounds, the fireplace illuminating him. Some furniture was covered in blood. There was a large wound covered by his hand, but it looked like he was unable to control the blood pouring from his stomach, and my sister Sarah standing above him, glaring down at him with a frightening grin that stretched ear to ear as she reached down to finish him.

I went to move to stop this madness. My mind was racing. What was my sister doing? How did she do that to Chris? He is a renown warrior, the strongest of us all. But before I could reach them and separate them, Amanda flashed into my vision and grabbed me by my throat, pinning me against the wall with supernatural strength. I couldn't understand her beautiful eyes. They looked wrong, corrupted by something demonic. Her eyes were jet-black, but I could feel them piercing through my soul as if she was savoring a meal to come.

Her grip tightened around my throat. I thought my world was going to go black. I saw Terry burst in from a side room screaming something inaudible, and flames bursting from an amulet in his hand. Amanda and Sarah's screeches were so loud my ears felt like they were bursting. But instead of the flames engulfing them, they seemed to bend around us but started a fire on the walls around us. Amanda dropped me and turned to my older brother Terry. I fell to the ground with a loud thump. I could feel the air rushing back into my lungs, which were in more pain than I could imagine with my almost crushed throat. I looked up and saw my sister Sarah grabbing Chris and looked like she was biting his neck. His strength seemed to leave him as she wrapped herself around him like a python squeezing her prey. His cries left his throat as it looked like blood was pouring from her mouth. I could hear my two siblings fighting one another when I heard a loud thud. I glanced over to the see Amanda coiled around Terry, biting deep into his neck; shock consumed his face.

"Jason, we need you—" I tried to say but was unable to. Where was Jason? I kept thinking. I wanted to cry out for him but I couldn't. My body wouldn't listen to me; I was terrified. Tears poured from my eyes in shame that I could not save them from these monsters. Terry's eyes seemed so scared as she gorged herself on him. Then out of nowhere, a hand yanked me up and I came face-to-face with a man looking more beast than a man—eyes darker than the night, teeth so razor sharp it would rip my flesh off with ease. His facial structure looked more beast than a man also. He was insanely muscular. I could feel his anger as he looked into my eyes; his breath smelled foul. And then he turned, and, with all of his might, threw me through the air.

I grunted as I burst through the front door, skidding into the front yard. My body was wracked with pain. Cuts everywhere. Blood following from my forehead. I went to get up on my knees, hunched over, gasping for air, for the nightmare to end, but this pain...this blood dripping onto the ground. How can it feel so real in a dream? This isn't happening.

Then a voice from inside the door, almost growling said, "No, boy, this...this is reality..." The body coming into my blurred vision, his body covered in black short fur was almost more wolf than man. His steps seemed heavy as each step he took left a deep paw print. It walked out of the shadow of the house into the moonlight, but a strange, almost black smoke, lightly came off his fur. His deep growl seemed to echo through my head like a lion purring in my ear.

I struggled up to one knee and looked up and saw the moon high in the sky; it was dark red: the blood moon, and in its wake, the village burned. Screams filled the air then the smell, the gore, and the sound of battle filled the night sky. Quinn filled my mind, but I struggled both to my feet and face My aggressor.

My vision was blurred; my body was wracked with pain, but I must stand. I must save Quinn and my family. I yelled, "What have you done to them?"

His laugh was deep and slow. "Whatever do you mean? They are my family now. I gave them the gift of the Blood Moon. It changes everyone differently. It makes it exciting, don't you think? One bite from me and they become my children. Who knows what they will become?" And another growling laugh came from him as if he was enjoying all of this.

"You're a monster. Damn you." It hardly got out of my strained throat.

"Come then, boy. I hope you put a better struggle than your brothers. Better yet...why not join me? Don't die here and live forever with your family. I see it in your eyes. You want to say yes. Give in now! Or die here, it matters not to me."

My mind was racing after hearing his word echoing through me. I could hear my once loved city turning to hell around, and there was nothing I could do to stop it. The rain started to fall all around me. "I can't!" I yelled. "I won't let this happen." I roared!

He opened his long arms in acceptance of my challenge. I charged across the muddy ground, my fists balled tight. I roared as I closed the distance. The monster didn't even try to dodge the punch as I threw everything I had into it. I leaned into and felt pride as it crashed into its jaw. I heard cracking, but then I quickly reeled in pain as it was my hand that had been broken. And as I huddled over, I couldn't see the strike to my stomach as I went flying to the ground. Pain washed over me. My cries filled the air. I looked up and saw him staring at me, grinning so wide. I hate that grin.

He picked me up with one arm; his strength is unreal. And he looked over to my burning house and pointed and said, "Look."

Shadows started walking out, my sisters first. They looked dark, pale skin. But their faces were twisted; blood covered their faces. Tears ran from my eyes as they elegantly walked toward me.

Sarah giggled so cheerfully as she saw me. "Ohhh, William, look at what you did to your hand." Sarah glanced over to elder sister who walked over with such elegance. Her arms coiled around her sister's waist as her dark eyes poured over me. Her smile looked sinister. Two pointed fangs poked out on the edge of her smile, still covered in blood.

"Look at his condition, sister," Sarah said with a sad tone.

Amanda leaned her head on her sister's shoulder. "Look at little William," she bit out. "So strong, so proud, so weak."

The words felt like slaps to the face when she said them. "Let us save you, little brother. Join us. Let just be one *big* family." I wish I could explain this feeling. Words felt like venom running through me as they both start to giggle in a disturbing way that made my stomach sick. Then in the background, I heard someone stumbling toward the door.

My oldest brother clutched the door, wrecked doorframe. His body was trembling as he struggled to stand, his other hand holding his stomach. The sight of him gave me hope.

"You think I would fall so easy," he bit out, blood rolling down the edge of his lips. But as soon as he stepped forward, his weight dragged him to his knees. I tried and spoke but nothing came out. The rain started to crash around us; the mighty warrior lurch's up, roaring as if something was tearing him apart. The sight was horrifying as his screams ripped through me. His hands grabbed at his clothes and ripped them off then steam started to pour from his eyes, causing him to screech in agony. His body started to grow larger before us, his skin turning into grayish color. His long black hair fell out in chunks, and soon my brother looked like a Titan in front of me.

Tears rolled out of my eyes like waves crashing against a beach. His eyes were blood red, almost glowing. His body rose and fell with each breath, releasing steam from his mouth. The creatures before as well as me stared in awe of his presence like you can feel the pressure his body gave off.

But soon, I looked away to hide my weakness and saw the battle still raging in the streets of the town. And almost like a shadow hugging me, Sarah's head suddenly was next to me, almost rubbing against mine. But I am trying to spot the creature who attacked me. He must have disappeared behind my brother. My heart was racing as she grabbed my face, squeezing it tight.

"Come on, little brother, do die like the rest of vermin then, brother."

"I... I ca—" I tried to say something, but her hand was grasping my chin with a powerful grip. Then she slowly brushed her pointer finger against my chin.

She giggled, which made my world feel like it slowed down, and with her very energetic voice, said, "Well...too bad, brother, I wasn't asking." Her hand ripped my head back and bit down so hard on my neck it blinded my vision with pain. I tried to yell out, but nothing will come out. My eyes grew wide as the moon seemed to pulsate a howl and filled my ears as I heard voice call out to me, telling me to give in, but I couldn't. I roared back though it's only in my mind.

A booking gurgled laugh filled my being and a deep voice was telling me, "Never for long, the blood moon." I felt its power like it's consuming me. When the crest growl pushed me away just as an arrow came soaring through the air, it hit her in the leg. Her yell was like a screech that seemed to make your brain feel like it's exploding.

My body went straight to its knees, trembling and weak. Time slowed down, and I looked around and I hear voices yelling for me to run, Amanda grabs Sarah as he is yelling "you Bastard" to someone, and in an instant, they vanished into thin air, which I couldn't understand how they did that. I looked up and saw about twenty of our soldiers and Jason with his long bow, grabbing at me and yelling for me to run.

I saw the large Titan was slow to react, but when he did, he dashed forward, trying to grab me, and Gustav and another warrior blocked his path. I yelled, "No!" I was picked up, and we started to run when my oldest brother spoke finally.

It's slow, but it deepened and boomed, "Ahh, William, why run away? It's useless. I will hunt you wherever you go. You would let these men die for you to escape?"

The question hit me hard. Running like a coward is something I've never done when it comes to a fight, but this is not the same.

Gustav pointed his large blade to his former chief, drawing the attention of the Titan. "Let's see if I still have anything that can still teach you, boy," provoking his rage. But before I could see the first swing thrown, Jason launched me to my feet, and we took off down the hill with the other the warriors. I could hear Chris laughing and yelled, "Run, brothers, run."

Down the hill, Jason, myself and a mix rag tag group of his personal guard and town watch who all look like they walked through hell. The first bodies I saw are folks I have seen before but then a creature lay next to them.

"Jason!" I cried out, "what is this? It looks like some kind of ghoul. Its face look human but diseased."

"That's what has been swarming the city," one soldier called out. Another walked up; they took us completely by surprise because they came from inside the city. We got trapped, and soon our aim was to protect the citizens. The war-torn man looked down and started to cry, "It was a bloodbath," gripping his sword.

"We must move," another called out. "There are still pockets of men left, but if we are to escape, we cannot linger."

"We cannot leave men behind. These are our comrades and people," I roared as I looked over to Jason and him over at me, and I could see the panic in his eyes. He drew an arrow so fast and sent it flying past me. I hardly had time to lean back as it went clean through a ghoul behind me, holding a blade ready to strike me down.

The force of the arrow sent its head into the wall behind him. Jason ran over to him and yelled in a serious tone, "Do you see this?" as he pointed down to the dead ghoul. "They are turning the rest of the people here into these damn things!"

Then we heard a loud roar from up on the hill, sending a chill through us all. I looked down and felt more anger running through me for what was happening.

"Did you see Quinn, brother?"

"No, I haven't. We got separated early on, but don't worry, she can take care of herself."

I started to rub my neck. I remembered the bite mark. Fear ran through my mind about what I could become. The man they seem to follow did say each bite affects everyone differently. Who knows it might not have an effect on me. Hope ran through my mind but was cut off quickly as Jason handed me a sword and yelled for me to keep moving. I didn't hesitate and took off after them. Shortly after making their way through the streets of dead mothers, fathers, sons, daughters, soldiers and ghouls alike, bodies twisted in embrace struggling even after death. I remember each face and hear their screaming, filling my mind. We soon made it to the main gate as I caught up with the rest of the group, which had stopped dead in their tracks.

Jason and I pushed to the front to see a hundred dead soldiers and citizens scattered about the courtyard. I looked over and saw Terry, my second oldest brother, leaning against the wall, wiping blood from his hands and behind him, a group of ghouls. He was staring at us with contempt. After a long moment, he finally said, "Well, looks like this is the end for you, William." Then he noticed Jason in the group. "Oh, Jason, where have you been? You have missed the party. Late like always, I suppose."

Jason blew off the taunt and launched an arrow at Terry, but it burst into flames and scattered like the wind before it reached him.

"Aww, good try, Jason, but better luck next time, I guess," he said in a sarcastic tone.

I glanced over at Jason who was clearly uneasy about this brother's newfound abilities. I took a few step toward him. "Terry, please, what are you doing? This isn't you! Whatever that monster did to you, we can reverse it! You of all people can! You know magic, right? Please come with us, brother. Save our family, please!"

Terry looked hard at him for a moment then looked at the blood moon and laughed, clapping his hands all the while. "Well said, little brother, but I have to refuse your offer. I seem to like this new me," raising his arm as fire rushed around his hand, engulfing it. "This new me has so much more...potential as well. I can feel my sickness leaving me. But time has run short it seems. You should have come with us, brothers, when you had the chance. The girls will miss you, William, when you're gone." Then he looked over at Jason. "Well, not so much you since you did shoot one in the leg. Is that how you treat your sisters? I am sure they would love to get their hands on you. The room you sent many men to die can be yours as well, how fitting."

Jason laughed and replied, "Tell our sisters they will be waiting for a while longer. I don't plan on dying here today."

Terry grinned from ear to ear and said with a voice that could only be described as dreadful: "Kill them all."

Ghouls of all kinds, horrific forms, poured from the gate. Jason and I both looked at each other, knowing this might be the end. In the moment, deep inside of me, courage burst within, and with my battle cry, I charged head straight into the howling groups of monsters, ahead with Jason, and his men at my back.

The first creature charged straight at me, howling some inaudible tones at me as he swung just too high as I evaded under the strike, launching my body, shoulder first, knocking the monster over on its back and thrust my long sword deep into the stomach of my enemy. Both of us went flying and tumbled over for several feet as I landed on top of him, feeling all the air go out of his lung. I plunged it deeper into its stomach; the beast bellowed in pain as blood rushed from the wound and coughed as it choked on blood in its throat.

As I rose up, I pulled my sword out of the gut of the lifeless figure. Time slowed down when our eyes met, and I felt just a small bit of vengeance for what had happened here today. I looked around and saw the other soldiers clashing in the shadow of the gate. I saw one soldier went down as two ghouls jumped at him and tore into his arms and legs with their razor-sharp teeth ripping large amounts of flesh away, blood gushing everywhere. His screams were deafening.

In that moment, out of the corner of my eyes, I saw a ball of spikes coming right at my face. My senses snapped back and dodged just to the side, just in time for it to barely scrape my head as the maul went past as a big ghoul with a massive spiked ball on a chain pushed past me. The hulking mass stumbled and regained his balance, but when he did, it's too late. I am already on top of him, slashing high and low, cutting around the upper arm and abdomen. The festering smell of the wounds stung my nose as it stumbled backward. The creature roared as it tried to dodge my fast strikes. But its reaction was too slow and I caught the tip of the blade on the throat of the creature, and dark blood splattered all over the ground.

It fell over, clutching its throat, trying to stop it, but seconds later, it's lying, still lifeless. I did not have time to catch my breath when I heard Jason calling out orders to some of the remaining soldiers that were alive. Jason was dropping the hell spawns left and right with his blazing fast arrows. I always thought my brother was second rate, but in this moment, watching him fight, I truly admired him. Then I looked over at a man crying out as he was getting overwhelmed by five ghouls. My heart began to race as I watched him being slashed at by their sharp claws and their snapping jaws. He fought with desperation when one beast lunged for his leg and cut a large gash in his thigh with a blade it grabbed off the ground. He started to stumble as he roared in pain but was quickly rushed by the other savage beasts and thrown to the ground and ripped apart.

I should have moved to help him, but I was afraid, mesmerized by the insanity of what was happening, when they lost interest in the lifeless man lying beneath, when one suddenly spotted me and rushed at me. His face was covered in thick blood and covered in blind rage, rushing at me on all four limbs to give it more speed.

But as it lunged right at me, I rolled to the left, barely escaping the deadly beasts' grasp. I hardly recovered my balance when two more barreled into me with so much force. It sent me flying into a wall, knocking the wind out of me. I rushed to get back, but all five beasts surrounded me. Panic filled my mind. The ghouls hissed as they slowly closed in around me. Inching their way closer to me, each one of those black eyes only focused on the kill. Me...they want me... I looked around to see if anyone was close enough to help. But I was alone; everyone was in the struggle of their lives. I saw Jason on the wall, tangling with a big ghoul like I had dealt with earlier. The monster was holding onto a very large sword, but he was just fast enough to avoid a deadly strike. But I didn't have time to worry about them. I was in a bad position myself.

When I felt something drawing my gaze up into the sky, the blood moon seemed to get bigger and more powerful than before, even with all the fighting, the cries from humans and hellish monsters, and the storm that raged. Nothing mattered to me at this moment but the moon. Its light seemed to be pouring into me like an infection spreading into my veins. All the anger, all the rage, all the pain seemed to explode inside of me.

The five ghouls sensed something and rushed at me with a fearsome roar. They all jumped the last few yards, ready to tear me apart! My world seemed to spin. Time slowed down as my right arm seemed to explode. I screamed so loud and doubled over as my anguish filled my right arm. I looked down to see my arm transforming into this demonic arm. It's larger than my left. The skin seemed to die and turned completely black. Large red veins started budging beneath my skin. I was struggling to breathe, and tears rolled from my eyes. Pain shot out like a wave down my arm. My hands looked more like a wolf with no fur. My fingernails turned sharp as I yelled out. This couldn't happen to me! I must save my family. *I wouldn't become your slave!* I bellowed from deep within myself. I resisted the change with all my might. My body shook horribly. But as I knelt, hunched over, the first ghoul slammed his massive body into mine, pushing me against the wall with a loud thump. Deep inside of me, the power of the blood moon rushed over me and I raised my new arm so fast into the large ghoul it was lifted off the ground and I sent it flying into two of the other beasts, knocking them down.

The other two smaller ghouls just to the left of me kept rushing straight at me. I launched myself forward with a loud battle cry. My demonic fist connected with the jaw of the first monster, breaking the lower jaw straight off its head. Blood and teeth cracked from the sheer force, then as I threw a second strike into its chest of the beast sending it flying back through the air, dying before it even hit the ground. As I went to turn, the other creature charging me, I felt it jumping onto my back and wrapping itself around me, and pain washed over me as its teeth sank into my shoulder. Blood flowed freely out as he bit harder. I bellowed in pain and fell backward, slamming the monster into a wall, feeling his head crack against the wall. I felt its grip loosen just enough for me to break it and turn and slam my fist into its stomach, piercing its gut. I looked at the ghoul's eyes and watched them widen with shock with what just had happened. I grinned as I saw the life in its face leave it. I gripped my hand out, pulling its intestines out, blood splattering all over my legs, but it didn't matter to me.

I went to look back for the other two ghouls left, but they had already ran. I smirked, feeling unstoppable. I looked over and saw my shoulder had already stopped bleeding. *That's good,* I thought to myself. If Sarah didn't bite me, I would have been ripped clean through.

I looked up at the blood moon. As the pain started to wash over me again, The agony was worse than before. I fell down, gripping my new demonic arm, and I couldn't understand, but it's transforming back to normal. I could hear and feel each bone cracking back into its normal place. The pain was unreal. I choked out a scream, but the pain had seemed to take the breath away from me, and in seconds, it's back to a normal human arm.

What was I thinking? What does this mean for me? I got back up, surrounded by dead warriors and monsters. The battle still raged on when I remembered Terry was around. I looked frantically over to see if I could find Terry by the gate, but he was gone. I started scanning the battlefield to see where he is hiding, but it was too late. I heard his voice behind me. "Your new strength is impressive, BUT YOU ARE TOO SLOW, LITTLE BROTHER!" he yelled.

I could feel the heat rising on my lower back and a shock wave that blew me clear to the other side of the gate. My ears were ringing so loud, and my back felt burned badly. My clothes melted into my skin. It's too painful to even move. But I struggled to get up as Jason cut down two ghouls to reach me by the front gate. His hand reached down to mine, slowly helping me up. Every inch I moved was agonizing. My muscles felt like dead weights. I felt so weak and useless. My mind was confused about what just happened. As I looked around, there was fire everywhere, and in my mind, I wondered how I was not dead and turned into a crisp. Even more bodies were added to the mass that was already here. The smell was foul. Burning it made my stomach churn. Countless bodies were lying on the ground: their eyes black, their teeth bloodied from combat, some missing arms, legs, and heads. I looked around and noticed it was only Jason and myself left; the rest of Jason's men were burned, lying on the ground. Some were so burned I couldn't make out some of the faces—nothing but charred skin.

We led them to their deaths. I felt deeply wounded for how brave they fought to only die in the end. But there, Terry was leaning against the fountain surrounded by the dead, looking at us with a deadly serious expression but also looking as if he was studying us with those glasses, fully knowing there were those black eyes behind that was tearing us apart limb from limb.

"You know that I should have killed you both with the rest of your men," Terry said with an annoyed tone. "I guess Sarah got too over eager. Biting you has had a significant effect on how durable you are even without that arm of yours. How interesting that your change is only temporary. I wonder if it can bring back out..." His eyes slowly left me and stared at Jason, deadly eyes. "Jason, you just got lucky," he said in a low tone. "How long will that last you through before you die?"

I was struggling to even keep up on my feet, let alone my eyes open. And the damn ringing in my ear made it hard to hear what was going on. But as Terry was walking forward to what seemed like the end for us, his body seemed to glow with fire engulfing the world around us. I thought this was the end, all the struggling we went through to only be in vain, killed by our own brother.

But in that instant, Quinn appeared and faced my youngest brother, her amulet glowing bright flames bent around us.

"Quinn!" I roared, but her eyes were glowing with white light the barrier she shields us with quickly starts to crack under the pressure of his spell. She roared out, pushing her body to her limit.

Then she looked back at me over her shoulder. "Sorry I took so long this time and kept you waiting. I helped another group get out."

I tried and walked to her, but the energy leaking from her body shoved me and Jason back. The shields cracked even further as a black void appeared from behind us. Quinn saw it as well as us and held out her hand to grab mine, but as the void engulfed us, I saw my sisters shatter the barrier and knock Quinn down, her screams filling my ears. The world seemed to vanish. In a flash, we were thrown on the ground with hard smack, knocking the wind out of my chest. I barely had the strength to open my eyes when I looked up to see a short lady with long brown hair in very classy clothes. It was hard to make out any real description. She looked over to an older man with some type of armor covering his whole body. Was he a knight? Where was he from? *What the hell is going?* was what was running through my mind.

"Quinn," I tried to say, but no words came out, and all I could hear before I passed out from the old man was "Well, looks like we got them out someone out just in time."

CHAPTER 2

Wake of the Rising Storm

"Wake up!"

What? Am I dreaming again?

"Wake up!" And with a painful jab to my side, my eyes snapped open. "William! It's me, Jason. Wake up. We gotta go, man."

"Ugh…" I tried to push myself up with my arms, but my strength was down to its last leg.

"Whoosh! Man, take it easy."

Each inch I raised myself off the ground seemed like I was lifting a dead weight. I looked up and saw my older brother looking down at me with an exhausted face. I studied him. There were small cuts on his outfit. There was blood all over his arms. I asked him if he was okay.

He looked at me with a smirk. "Well, a lot better than you, I imagine."

I managed a small laugh. "So where are we?"

Jason looked down the mountain. "Honestly, not far away from the city. I can see the city burning still." He tried to say Quinn's name, but I held my hand up to show him that it's too much for me to think of.

He sighed. "It's over." He looked down and held back his anger. "All my men…" Tears rolled down his face. "Damn it!" He yelled. "What the hell is going on? What were those things?"

A voice from behind me made me jerk away as I pushed myself to my feet. "It's a plague of sorts I suppose." The figure that was talking came into view more clearly. It was the knight with crude steel armor, leather pants with soldiers boots with a big shield that had two lions on facing one another as if they were about to fight. He was tall, probably four inches taller than me. But smaller than Chris by a large margin. His sword gleamed in the dim light with a red ruby in the hilt. It was amazing-looking. He had a rough cut, gray hair that slightly hung over his face, clean shaven, brown eyes, with a scar that ran from his cheek to his chin.

"What is your name, knight?" I blurted out finally. He looked off at the burning village.

I waited a moment, thinking he was ignoring me, and as I went to ask him again, he looked at me with a low tone and said, "Yeah, I heard you. My name is Felix. This is Annie." And a young girl walked out from behind him, probably around my age, about 5'5". She got long brown hair, a thick jacket that was unbuttoned with a red shirt, brown jeans, and boots.

"Hi, guys. You both looked in bad shape when you came through the portal I opened up! Y'all should be thankful I got wicked talent with bandages." And she smiled big.

Felix put his hand on her head and smirked. "Yeah, yeah. You're Miss Talent all right, toothpick."

She looked up at him and gave him an angry face and said under her breath, "I should have teleported you down to the town."

My eyes widened then. "Why didn't you save Quinn?"

"Who?" she asked. "Oh yes, the girl with the barrier. You should be thankful she saved you men."

We both looked down in shame. "So you saved us, little girl?" Though it came out more rude than expected.

The girl named Annie looked over at us and got real loud. "Who you calling a little girl! And yes, for what its worth, I did save you, but I think I am already regretting it."

"The questions keep piling up," Jason pronounced.

"But for now, I don't think it's a good idea to stay here, Felix."

"Hmm, agreed," said Felix. "We got a camp not too far way with other knights. I hope you're ready to go. It won't be an easy travel" as he grabbed a large bag of supplies.

"Those beasts can be anywhere. Well, we gotta go anyways. Might as well not waste time," said Jason.

I looked at Felix as he went to turn and walk away. "Why should we trust you?"

He didn't even look back to answer me. "Look, if it wasn't for us, you would be dead with the rest. I wouldn't have wasted my time saving you if it wasn't for a good reason. I don't have time to explain now, but if that interests you, then come. If no, die here in this forsaken land. But we are moving now."

Jason put his arm on my shoulder. "Let's go, little brother." I nodded and went to start walking away but glanced just over at our home one last time. "I will come back to save you," I vowed, looked forward, and started after them.

Seems like a full day had passed when daylight was shining through the trees again. I felt its rays on my skin. I didn't remember it feeling so damn good before.

"Hmm, how much longer 'til this camp, Felix?" I said with a tired tone.

He took a few moments and thought to himself. "Well, I think we should make it by nightfall."

Jason laughed. "What, little brother? Not used to a good hike?"

I gave him a shove. "Stop being a jerk, Jason."

He laughed. "Don't be such a child."

I looked at him with a little bit of irritation. Jason kept laughing, and then up ahead, Annie came over a tall rock. "Hey! Will you two get a room already?"

Jason and I both looked at her with angry faces. Annie burst out laughing. "Look at you two. You both are so much more fun to mess with than Felix." Then she looked at the big knight. "He is like a rock."

Felix ignored the insult and looked at me. "Hey, there is a creek up ahead. We will get more water there."

Hmm, water sounds so good right now, seemed like a lifetime since I had some. "Okay," I pronounced, "let us keep moving" when suddenly, a loud crack in the distance was heard. We all stayed quiet, listening for any signs of the things following us. After a long pause, we didn't hear anything. Felix said in a low voice, "It's time to go," and pointed in the direction he wanted to go.

Jason led the way, stealthily moving down the forested valley to the creek Felix pointed to. My mind was racing, wondering what was possibly following us. Was it his recently turned family? Anyone of them would be horrible at this moment. Jason and I were both exhausted after last night.

About twenty minutes later, we reached the creek we were heading for. We heard no further noises possibly following us.

"Honestly," said Felix, "it's too quiet."

Annie looked up at the knight and snared in a low voice, "Don't say that. Have you ever heard of bad luck?"

He looked down at her and smiled. "No, toothpick. Luck is for the weak."

Honestly, that seemed like something my oldest brother would say. And it struck me wrong at heart, but I let it slide off. There was not the time for it.

Jason came down from one of the trees, looked at Felix, and whispered, "It looks clear. If we are going to refill our water, we gotta be quick. We will be the open for a good minute."

Felix nodded and turned to us. "Okay, guys and toothpick, we gotta make this quick and get to the other side. Don't drag ass, okay? We don't know what's around here." We all nodded and followed Felix led out of the woods into the creek bed at a good jog.

After about fifty yards out, we made it to the creek bed and started taking out our containers to fill up with water. I was staring at the water; it was so clean. My hands were so dirty, still had the faint irony smell of blood. When we saw the water shaking with each step, I already knew who it was when we heard a booming voice which seemed to come from everywhere. "Cowards, always running."

My heart sank like an anchor. I looked over a Jason. His eyes were wide. You could see the sweat on his brow. Annie was next to Felix who now was drawing his sword. Then Chris's booming voice rang our ears once again. "Come out, boys, your big brother misses you," which was followed by a demonic laugh.

I stood up, trying to spot him, then out of the woods where we came from, his monster stature appeared at almost 6'9" now and large muscles. His hair seemed to be completely gone, and now there was some type of tattoo on his head that seemed to glow. His huge battle axe looked even more deadly than before. My heart began to pump so hard and fast. I thought it was going to pop from my chest.

Ghouls started creeping from the wood line about fifty yards away, had to be almost thirty of them. The odds alone with that, but with them, it's looking grim.

Felix walked out of the creek bed, standing straight up, grabbed his bag, and threw down a bundle of arrow to Jason and a spare blade to me. He looked like a man ready to die. You could feel him drawn to this fight as he grabbed a large shield off his back. And here I am, looking over the ground, looking at my big brother. "Damn it! Stand up, coward. You're stronger than this."

Jason walked up next to me. "Come on, man. Looks like we aren't running from this one, right?"

I smacked his hand away. I summoned my courage. "Yeah, not this time." I looked my brother in the eyes. "You got my back, right?"

He laughed. "Isn't that my line?" And he stepped forward.

"Annie!" Felix yelled. "You know what you have to do. I know you're already strained out from the portal, but if we are going to beat this guy, you need to pull out something quick."

She looked at the big knight and looked at Chris and put her hands together and closed her eyes. Some type of energy started pouring around her, and she yelled as if strained from all the concentration and looked at me. "Hey, William, I am going to need some time! I need time to keep them off my back or we are toast!"

I gripped my long sword in my hand till I was white in the knuckles. Felix looked at me with an excited eyes. "You ready to fight, boy?"

I looked at him and said with a serious voice, "I will see you on the other side." And from the other side you could hear Chris's booming battle cry as the ghouls rushed at us, ready to take our lives. Jason's arrows were already dropping the creatures long before they even got to us. I was readying my stance when Felix dashed forward with impressive speed for a man of his age. The first ghoul rushing on all fours jumped in the air and came down with a slash of his deadly claws. But instead of cutting into Felix's flesh, it met his big shield that went crashing to its face, cracking bone as if hit an unmovable wall with full force. The beast blood smeared against his shield and fell to the ground but just as the beast went to get up from its daze. Felix roared and stomped his boot down on; its head so hard its skull splattered all over the rocky ground.

I saw Felix in the thick of the fight. When three charged at me, one got hit by Jason's arrow before even reaching me. The next two attacked at once. I grunted as one's claws glanced my side, but as it's going by me, I swung my sword down with a loud roar. My sword cut straight through the spine of monster. It yelped in pain as it went tumbling past me and skidded to a halt and died.

As I went to look back, the second beast's fist connected with my face, knocking me clean of my feet. As I hit the ground, my head smacked a rock, almost making me black out. I went to struggle back up, but the monster pinned me to the ground. The world slowed down as I saw the claws coming at my face. I started to bring my arm up to block. But before the final blow could reach me, an arrow pierced the skull of the beast that towered over me and fell on top of me, his lifeless black eyes staring into mine. I saw Jason running up to me and pulled the body off when my world finally stop spinning, but I don't even thank Jason after he helped me up. I saw Felix tangling with a few more half-breeds and crushing them with his shield and cutting another one down with his amazing sword. But all I could think of is Annie! I looked back to where I left her and she looked scary. More energy was pouring out of her body, like a whirlwind was around her. Her eyes were all white, and she was chanting some inaudible spell. But I could see a half-breed rushing toward her!

I instantly sprang into action, rushing toward her! I don't know if I am going to make it in time.

The beast went to jump at her. But as it did, its skin started to melt! It hit the ground early and leaped back and so did I when I started to feel the heat coming from her. I looked at the beast, and all the skin from the monster's elbow and down was melted; its grasping its arm in pain as Jason's arrow strikes it right between the eyes. I looked back at him. And he looked at me and yelled, "I wouldn't get any closer to her. She looks unstable."

Annie was openly yelling now. I guessed she would be able to use her spell soon. When I felt the ground shake, I jerked my head over to see Chris charging in with rage in his eyes. Felix quickly killed the half-breed that was around him and jumped in the way to block his path to Annie. I started to run up to help Felix when Chris swung his mighty battle axe at the old warrior. He brought his mighty shield up to block the hit. I yelled for Felix to dodge! But he stood his ground. Both warriors roared, giving it their all, as one blow could decide the whole fight. The axe collided against his mighty shield. A loud boom echoed off the shield, throwing dust and rocks into the air. The sheer hit sent a shock wave that you could feel hit you; it was unreal. How could anyone survive that? But as the dust settled, Felix was well intact. His shield was dented but not broken from the swing.

Chris took a jump back, looking at the new opponent in amusement. When he spoke, his words felt like they were inside of your head. "Well," Chris boomed, "that shield is sturdy, but how long can you hide behind it before I break it?" And with that said, Chris launched another offensive with a high strike so fast Felix was hardly able to bring the heavy shield up to block. The blow hit so hard it brought him to his knees. Chris bellowed a roar and went to strike again, but before he could, Felix lunged his body forward, crashing his shield against the massive body of Chris, pushing him back ever so slightly. To give him room to swing his large sword that cut along the demon warriors' ribs, Felix pushed past him a couple of yard and turned with his shield raised, expecting the death machine to be on him, but he was just standing still.

I was watching the duel in amazement. Most of the half-breeds were dead or scattered back into the tree line, afraid to get in the path of the demonic warrior, then the ground seemed to shake again. Chris bellowed out in roar as it looked like steam was coming from eyes. It was terrifying. Chris's physic seemed to be in top shape. The wound on his ribs was incredibly starting to heal again. Was his rage really that powerful that he can heal himself with it? What more powers does he have? Do we even stand a chance?

Then Jason grabbed me and yelled to Felix, "We must attack him all at once!" He yelled at the top of his lungs. He couldn't reach Annie at all cost! Felix nodded, and I summoned the strength to face my brother head on. I saw Felix charged back in as Chris turned to face the warrior. An arrow struck him in the shoulder, not even fazing him. Another arrow hit in the leg. Felix dodged left as the massive axe slammed next to him, almost throwing him to the ground from the force. I charged in from behind, surprising the demonic warrior and slashed his lower leg and upper back.

Chris roared in rage. Inside, I was feeling amazed in that I landed a strike on the man he called his brother. Felix followed up with another attack, thrusting with multiple strikes and could hardly land a strike as the demon barely brushed past them. I sensed an opportunity to attack again and rushed forward. But as I did, Chris's massive axe slammed into Felix's large sword, almost breaking it with such speed, sending him soaring right into me with enough force we both get knocked to the ground. With Felix's large frames on top of me pinning me to the ground, I could hardly breath.

I choked out, "Can you get off of me?"

Felix smirked and pushed off of me. We both got up to our strained legs and regained our balance. I looked at Felix. Blood was flowing from his forehead. His breath was ragged. He looked at me and back at Chris. "What is he, William? This man has strength beyond this world."

Chris turned around, towering over both of us. Jason ran up next to us. He was out of arrows but still has two daggers on him. The demon warrior smirked, his red eyes glaring at us. "Looks like you can't run anymore!" He snarled. "You all will die by my hands."

I moved a few steps forward, challenging him. "Brother, no! You are the strongest man I know! Stop this madness," I yelled. "Why are you letting someone control you? Join us and fight this master of yours and return you back to normal."

He looked at me with a very blank face. "William, I am going to grind your bones into dust. Do you understand me? Unless you get stronger, none of you have a chance to win. I saw your arm change when you fought Terry. I would rip it from your body and watch you scream."

I lost all hope when his words hit me. How could he be so cruel? I glanced behind me. All the energy around Annie seemed to be focusing down into a ball of energy. The ground began to shake as Chris charged forward; his roar was thunderous. He lifted his battle axe high in the air, his eyes focused on me. "William, now you die!" he yelled as he jumped, slamming down his monstrous battle axe! I jumped back just in time to avoid it, but the ground under me shook so hard when his weapons connected with the ground. I lost my balance. I tried to dodge his next attack as he spun his massive leg so hard into my stomach. I thought most of my ribs had been broken. I went skidding almost twenty feet before coming to a stop. My lungs felt like they were exploding. I gasped for hair but could hardly breathe for a few moments. Once I regained my ability to breathe, I looked to see how Felix and Jason were faring the battle. Felix kept the demon busy with strong strikes and attacked with his shield landing a few clean blows.

Jason looked for an opening to make small cuts on him but kept his distance because with one clean shot, it could be the end for him. I looked over at Annie. She yelled for Felix to move. "I couldn't hold it any longer!" she yelled. Her body was shaking badly, I wondered how a girl like her was so powerful. Both Jason and I looked over to Annie, and in that slight moment, looking away from Chris, he took advantage of their mishap. Exploding with such speed toward Jason, the archer was surprised how he closed the distance on him so fast too he didn't have time to react. His massive hands thrust out and slammed into Jason's face, knocked him off his feet, but as he wracked, his body fell to the ground. The massive hand gripped around his skull and was twisted into the air as the demon threw him, soaring through the air like an arrow sending him crashing into a boulder with such force it made me sick to hear. I heard his scream as he smacked against the stone. Blood covered the rock where his head hit. He looked lifeless as he fell to the ground. My fears swelled in my chest. Panic entered my mind. I looked back and Chris, he once again used his ability to close the distance in an unreal pace and was already on top of Felix, but Felix's reflexes were on point. He brought his shield up just in time to avoid his fist, but instead of using his strength to break the shield, he grabbed his shield and ripped it out of the grasp of the veteran knight and sent it flying away. Felix was just down to his long sword which was nothing to count on.

Felix dashed forward, challenging the beast, both hand gripping his sword with all of his might. He brought his sword in an up slash motion, sending sparks flying off the stone as the sharp blade skidded across it. Chris looked down at the knight with arrogance and raised his none-weapon hand in a challenging motion. Felix seemed to be enraged by this and launched, swinging his sword so hard it could cut a man in half. Chris didn't even move away. And the sword pierced the abdomen of the monster-sized warrior. Felix pushed harder into, feeling his sword ripping through Chris's stomach. Blood poured out of the wound. His head rose in pain and roared that seemed to make the ground shake in fear.

Felix looked up under the shadow of the hulking man. "Die, you bastard!" he roared and went to pull out his long sword. But as he did, Chris's large hands grasped the blade itself and held it there. Blood flowed around the blade where he grabbed it and started to laugh. Felix, with all of his might, tried to yank the blade free but his grip was unreal. He looked up and saw Chris's glowing eyes looking down at him. He was grinning ear from to ear, his teeth razor-sharp. Steam started to pour from his eyes. His growl was deep, and he ripped out the sword from his body. Chris dropped his massive axe and sent his other hand lurching forward to grasp Felix's throat. He tried to dodge but was caught and launched into the air. Chris brought the knight to eye level, almost as if he was drinking the agony from him as he gasped for air. You could see the strain in his face. The blood vessels in his eyes started to bust under the strain. But in a last-ditch effort, he launched a kick that would break a normal man's jaw to Chris's chin. It hit with tremendous force but only cut Chris open slightly, but hardly even made him flinch.

I couldn't believe he was being choked to death by my brother, and there was nothing I could do. Each time I moved, my ribs felt like they will break even worse, but the whole world white out and in an intense flash.

Annie yelled something I couldn't understand, and a massive blast of wind and energy came from her. It seemed to tear apart everything in its wake. Chris looked surprised by the sudden deadly blast coming to him. He turned and threw Felix like a rag doll against the ground and faced Annie's attack. His roar was loud. He put his one arm up to block it! He was insane, even with all of this newfound strength. Could he stop such a thing? But as the blast hit his hand, it shoved him back. He struggled to stop the blast with one arm but after a few movements, started to get overwhelmed. He raised both arms to stop the blast. His war cry was loud and his muscles strained to stop it. I started to get hope that maybe we together had beaten this unstoppable force.

But just as it seemed we had won, when I saw a shadow flashed past me with lightning speed, I tried to make out the figure, and when I was finally able to see who it was, my jaw dropped. It's Sarah! Why was she even here? She looked at me with a deadly expression and put her hand on Chris, and they vanished into a black mist. The blast passed through and slammed into the side of the mountain where we came, and the explosion obliterated all the half-breeds that were watching from the forest. The shock wave knocked over trees for three acres in every direction. Wood splinters, rocks mixed with half-breeds fell everywhere around us. My ears were still ringing from the blast. I struggled to move forward in a daze. The world seemed to be rocking back and forth as I tried not to stumble over myself.

I stopped and took a deep breath. I noticed my ribs seemed to be healing better already. I gathered myself and steadily headed over to where I last saw my brother. The dust was thick in the air. I could hardly see what's in front of my face when there was a sudden pop as my broken ribs realigned itself. The pain from my ribs began to overwhelm me as the broken ones healed. I fell to one knee, and with my right arm, I grasped my ribs. I huddled over and spitted blood over my hands. The wind started to pick up as I saw a large figure coming my way. Fear rushed to my mind. My legs shake as I will myself up as the shadow becomes clear through my blurred vision the large knight walked up to me. He looked battered but still alive. His throat looked bruised badly from Chris's monstrous grip that was trying to squeeze the life from him.

"Are you okay, big guy?" I wheezed out.

He looked down at me with slight smile. "Yeah, I am fine, William." And he looked over to the body on his shoulder. He turned serious and looked back at me. "He needs a doctor soon or he might not make it." The news made my heart skip a beat. Felix looked past me with renewed worry. "Where is Annie?" His eyes were scanning the battlefield. He seemed to spot her and put down Jason and rushed off toward the creek bed.

I looked down at Jason. His head was bleeding badly. His breath was shallow. But he was still alive. I heard a noise from the direction Felix ran to. I reached down and grabbed Jason and threw him onto my shoulders. I smiled and thought to myself, *I am glad he is so light.* Anything heavier and my knees would break. I turned and started heading back to the creek bed. The dust was starting to settle now. I saw Felix holding Annie in a cradling position. I started to worry.

Felix looked back up at me. "She is fine," he said in a calm tone. "She only drained herself. She is asleep now. I suspect she won't be up for a day or so."

I managed a sigh of relief, but as I looked down at the girl, I couldn't help but wonder about this girl. Her abilities reminded me of Terry's. Was she infected also? I remembered before all of this magic, this world was weakened over the centuries and hardly even used anymore. Jason was right. The questions were piling up with not enough answers. Felix stood up, holding the small girl in his arms. He looked at me with curiosity. "I was guessing that bite on your neck is what saved you?"

I was caught off guard by the question. "I honestly don't know," I stammered. "The virus seems to only temporarily affect me, but I can feel it under my skin, scratching beneath the surface, like someone inside waiting to burst out."

The knight looked at me with worry. "You best keep it in check, boy. We need you to be alive for now, and if you look like you're a risk to Annie, I won't hesitate to end you."

The air was thick between the two of us as we stared at each other.

"Shut up, you big dumb knight," squeaked from the girl in his arms.

I looked down at her. "She was clearly dreaming about you big guys," I burst out. I could hardly hold the laughter back when a small giggle escaped my mouth. The knight growled and started to walk off, clearly annoyed by the girls dream.

"Hey, big guy! That wasn't my fault," I choked out between the laughter. "Come on! Wait up for me," as I started to walk off after him. *I hope this camp isn't too much farther away*, I thought to myself. The days had been too long, and we hadn't had any rest. Jason was still breathing, but I worried for him, but I pushed forward each step in front of the other. Each step brought a little more hope that we will be safe soon.

CHAPTER 3

The day had been long. We had only stopped a few times through the day to catch our breaths. The sun had been down for an hour or so already. My body was sore and I was sure Felix could smell me from a mile away.

"We are close now," the large knight said, snapping me out of the zone I was in. I sighed in relief as we walked through the woods. In the distance, you could see small torches on top of a large wooden wall surrounding the encampment. Relief washed over me like a warm water on a cold day. *Hold on, brother,* I said to myself. *We will get help for you.*

The large knight pushed out of the wood line to the wooden fort, cradling Annie in his large arms. I followed suit and stood next to him. There were two large towers overlooking the main gate. Two guards had their bows pointed right at us. One shouted down to us, asking us to identify ourselves.

Felix looked up at the guard with a scowl on his face. "You know damn well who I am."

The guard laughed. "I am just pulling your tail, you big lion. Don't get all snappy, will ya? Open the gate," he yelled.

The large wooden door cracked open.

"Hey!" I yelled up to the guard.

"Who are you?"

"No time to explain. We need a healer badly," I yelled up to the guard.

He looked down at us for a moment and gestured to the other guard next to him to go grab a healer. I started walking into the camp. Tents were set up around the camp, must be a hundred strong in this camp, men and women performing their duties, some sharping their weapons, other making arrows or securing their gear in preparation for what, I honestly didn't know. I heard Jason grumbling in his sleep when I heard from behind me, "Someone hurt?"

I turned as a tall woman came around the corner with three boys at her heels. She walked up to me, eyes focused on me. They were sharp eyes, a bright yellow, about the same height as myself. She had a blonde hair that ran smoothly down past her shoulder blades and a bandanna strapped around her forehead. She was wearing long leather pants and dark purple cloth shirt with fish-netted gloves.

"Hey!" she snapped at me, breaking my focus. "You rather let your friend die up there while you're busy staring at me?"

I blushed hard, knowing I was making a fool of myself. "He needs help," I quickly blurt out. "My brother took a blow to the head," I explained.

She pointed and the three strong boys took him from my shoulders and laid him on the stretcher. The woman went to walk away with her helpers. "Hey, where are you taking him, and what is your name?"

She looked back with her hair covering half of her face. "I am Iyana, and your brother is going to be fine. I will send someone to find you when he is better." And she ran off with her followers.

"William!" Felix called. He had two knights in black armor behind him. Both were sporting shields that had the same two lions on the shields as him. "It's time we introduce you to the leader of this group."

My mind was in so many places honestly. So much was going on it was hard to focus at the task at hand with Jason not by my side. But it was time to start making choices now. I nodded to the large knight and followed him through the large camp. As we were being escorted through, I saw plenty of soldiers sparing with one another. Then all of a sudden, my vision went blurry and pain shot down my right arm. I fell to my knees as I grasped my arm. My breath was turning ragged. "No," I snarled. I could feel the change trying to take over, the monster inside of me trying to rip through me. I couldn't focus on what was around me, but I am sure I could hear Felix arguing with someone. My body was shaking violently. My arm felt like it's about to explode. I couldn't change now. I couldn't die here. I roared within myself as I battled the primal desire within me.

Time seemed to slow down. Within moments, it seemed to pass. My arm stopped throbbing. My muscles taxed. I looked up and could see the tip of a blade point right at my face.

"William, are you okay?"

I couldn't make out the voice, but as I went to stand up, a young lady ran up, pushing the blade from my face and wrapped her arms around me. "You okay?"

I pushed the girl off and looked to see Annie staring at me. I managed a slight nod and raised to my feet. "I am fine." I was barely able to hold myself up.

One of the knight took off his helmet and looked at Felix. "You're responsible for him. If he starts to change again, you kill him. Is that understood?"

Felix looked at the dark knight and nodded his head and turned and started walking to the large tent in the center of the camp.

I tried to walk but almost stumbled forward. Annie jumped forward and wrapped my arm over her. I looked into her eyes. Did they ever seem so beautiful before?

"Let's go, silly mister. It's not wise to keep him waiting."

We started forward and I noticed everyone in the camp had stopped what they were doing and staring at me with uncertainty. I all of a sudden didn't feel so safe here.

"Don't worry. You just had us worried, William."

I breathed deeply, and with her help, we continued after the escort. We walked into the center of the camp, coming to a large tent. Felix was on one knee, bowed before a young man standing before him with two dark knights by his side. I moved over into the crowd to get a better look. The young man had spiked black hair, not as tall as me, wearing steel leggings, steel boots with fur around the cuffs. He wasn't wearing no breast plate and only spiked gauntlets. But he had an amulet around his neck that had a ruby lion that laid on his chest. He looked a little older than myself. But he seemed to radiate authority.

"Rise, knight," the leader said in an anxious tone. "Tell me what has happened to the Black Forge Estate. Is anyone alive?"

William looked over to me in the crowd and called me forward. I pushed my way forward through the crowd of knights and squires. I walked next to Felix and slightly bowed forward.

The leader looked at me with curiosity. "Who are you, sir?"

I looked around to Felix who was looking down at me and gestured for me to talk. I thought to choose my words wisely before I spoke since I didn't know who this man was. "Before I speak, I like to know who you are, and where are you from, and how do you know of my family's holding."

The leader smiled. "You are bold. I like that." His eyes were silver. His grin was seemingly cold. "I am Nicolai, prince and heir to the Dreathia Kingdom of the pride lands, just bordered just south of the Celica."

"Why are you here?" I said.

He looked as if thinking what was proper to say. "There is a rumor the dark forest holds a powerful stone that is unparalleled if held by the right man. I could stop this from spreading into other estates or even worse if we can't contain this."

I thought over his answer briefly. "I am William Blackforge, youngest brother to Chris Blackforge, chief of our land," I said to the prince.

"Continue," the prince replied.

"We were attacked. Most of my family besides Jason has been infected by a creature of sorts with what was called the blood moon virus. Chris and my other family members, backed by some foul monsters, slaughtered the villagers. Jason and myself barely escaped with our lives thanks to Annie and Felix. We were tracked down and attacked, but we seem to back my brother into a corner and he retreated, and now, well, here we are."

"And here you are," the prince repeated. His fist tightened, his jaw grinding as he turned around and looked to the moon. He slowly turned around and looked me in the eyes. "You are bitten, are you not?"

The weight of the question seemed to almost crush me. "I am," I replied.

The prince looked to the two large knights and nodded. Both, with surprising speed, rushed at me. I tried to launch myself back to avoid their grasp. I was exhausted. I was struggling to stay to my feet but quickly overwhelmed by their power forcing me to the ground. One knight grasped my head and yanked it up. I could see Annie trying to reach me, but Felix had already grabbed her and was moving her from sight. I looked at the prince. "What are you doing?" I tried to say as one of the knights' fists pummeled into my gut, knocking the wind out of me. I tried to yell for Jason as I grasped for air. I crumbled over. I couldn't see but I could hear heavy footsteps walking up to me.

"You're too dangerous!" I heard from the prince. "You cannot be trusted to be let free. Take him away out of my sight. Ready your troops, Commander. We march soon."

CHAPTER 4

Wakening of the Beast

A large storm was roaring outside. Lightning lights, the dark prison, cracks of thunder filled my ears, water dripped upon my head from the cracks in the ceiling. I couldn't sleep. I didn't know how much time had passed. The storm had been going for quite some time now, but it matters not.

My arms were pulled into the air by these damn chains. My feet were just barely touching the ground. My body was going numb from hanging here. I could feel the beast inside of me feeding on my despair like a vampire. I was so lost on the inside, confused I thought this was the right path.

I lifted my head, just enough to scan around the cell. The floor was hard, damp, and cold from the rain. There was one window with iron bars to my right. I was inside of a cage like an animal. I gritted my teeth in frustration for following blindly into this situation. I looked around once again. There was a single way in through a wooden door. I heard a few guards on the outside talking about the storm. My body was sore and bruised. My stomach was growling at me like an angry dog wanting food. They stripped me off my weapon and the little armor I had on. Now I was just in a damp cloth that covered me. I could almost hear the sky breathe in as another loud, thunderous boom filled the emptiness of my cell.

My brain seemed to waken from a groggy sleep when I thought I heard something move. My eyes looked at the dark shadows that looked like they were alive, creeping ever closer to their prey. When I heard something scrap along the wall in the darkness, my breath began to quicken. Slight giggle again from the shadows in the corner on the other side of the bars. My mind was groggy, but I wasn't crazy.

"Who is there?" I said weakly. No answer. I could feel eyes looking upon me, but who, I wondered.

"Annie, is that you?" I whispered. No answer. My mind began to race when a flash of lighting lit up some of the room. And when it did, a figure rushed back into the shadows before I could get a good look. "Who are you?" I asked again with more demanding tone. I could almost feel the shadows creeping up my back and gripping around my throat.

When in a flash, a shadow lurched out from the shadows and gripped the bars. I would have yelled if I had the energy, but all I could do was look straight into the dark pink eyes of a demon I once called my sister. Her eyes were focused on me. Her grin was wide, displaying two large fangs. She just stared at me, gripping the bars like she was drinking my pain. My body began to tremble, no way to protect myself. My worry was displayed over my face as I looked to the door and where I heard guards talking before. But now it's quiet. I could try and yell, I thought, but the storm was raging as it is. I would even be heard. I looked back at her, knowing I had to face this on my own, even in the situation I was in.

"How did you get in here?" I said hoarsely. Her eyes never broke contact with mine.

She looked excited to see me. "Dear…poor… William," she said in a soft voice. Her fingernails were sharp and seemed to curl around the iron bars as if they had a mind of their own. "I have missed you. I have been so bored just watching you, so I thought I would drop by and toy with you. I like the new girl. What's her name? Annie?"

My eyes drew narrow as I looked at her.

She noticed my reaction, and it seemed to fill her with joy. "I wonder what she would look like after I got my greedy hands around her throat."

My anger spiked after hearing my once innocent sister's words. She giggled once again and slowly walked to the cell door, looked at it, and with ease, broke the lock. It creaked as she almost glided into my cell. I tried to follow her movement when she disappeared behind me. My skin crawled as her sharp nails ran across my back.

"What do you want?" I said in an aggravated tone. I could hear her breathing quicken as her hand slid up around my throat and our eyes met as she came back in front of me. I tried to pull away as she pressed her forehead against mine. It was surprising and almost pleasant, after everything that had happened. Ironic that a sister and brother who once loved each other now both turned on the same day to beasts of another nature.

Her eyes seemed to grow bright pink. "I was to make you suffer, brother," she said in such a twisted slow voice. But she seemed sad, it was strange. Our eyes met again. Her eyes grew even more bright as if she had looked like she had figured out how to best make me suffer. Her face seemed to change from a pale beauty to a wicked demon as her grin stretched across her face. Her sharp tongue rolled over her fangs. She leaned in again, her mouth close to my ear. "I promise, brother, this is going to be fun. For me at least." Her head leaned back as the shadows around came alive. in a sudden the world seemed to become disoriented, dark, and cold. My shackles seemed to grow heavy and burn my wrists. I could feel bolts piercing my hands, my body hanging against a pillar.

I opened my eyes. Horror spread across my face. I was hanging above a lake of fire. I could feel fire licking the sweat from my body as it danced around me, burning my flesh till it boiled and charred. My cries to let me die were endless, but as my life would fade from me, I would always be brought back to life. My demonic sister overlooking me from the other side of the lake, Quinn kneeling by her side. Blood was coming from her eyes where her eyes used to be.

"Quinn!" I screamed but seemed like she could not hear me. Then flames would consume her as she danced around her to rhythm to my cries as if it was a song she enjoyed. It felt like eternity. I would beg for it to stop, swear at her, and my hate for her grew over time. But the pain, it never stopped. And all I could do was suffer in her hell she had created for me. Her damn giddy laughs would swarm my brain as I struggled to break my shackles, my rage ever growing. The beast inside consuming me after so long lost in my misery.

I looked across the river. She had stopped laughing, stopped dancing in her normal insane self. She looked over at me one more time, and in a black cloud, she vanished. My chains broke free and fell into the fire as I screamed. My body and mind was lost and everything was consumed by this fire. As I fell through the flames, darkness rushed around me once more. And my eyes jutted open, the pain was gone, but the hate remained; the eternal fire was gone. Sarah was gone. The cell door was open, and Quinn stood there, white energy glowing around her hands. She was crying.

"You saved me again." And a smile and tears ran across both mine and her faces. I remembered the moment I opened my eyes just before coming through the portal and there she was.

"Are you okay?" she said, wiping off the tears as she rushed to me. Her eyes were beautiful, her lips soft. She looked like an angel. She wrapped herself around me. I felt like I was coming to life again. A smile came over my exhausted face.

"I was lost for so long in a fire. I couldn't die."

"What do you mean? I don't understand, William. You've been here. What was happening to you?"

In my overwhelmed state, I looked around, and my vision came clear that it was Annie here and not Quinn. Panic filled me as I looked at her. "Where are the guards?"

She looked like she was pondering the question. She looked back up at me. I felt strange magic coming from her. I knew something was wrong. "When I got here, there were no guards."

"Can you get me down?" I said in a rush, but as I said, I knew something was wrong. The all too familiar laugh echoed around the room, followed by another one from another voice that was familiar—female. It was Amanda. Both here?

Lightning flashed, and I could see both figures leaning against the wall with smirks running across their devilish faces. Annie moved back to my left side. Her eyes focused on the two dark creatures.

"Annie, you must run."

Annie looked back up at me and smiled. "You best not take me lightly."

Sarah purred as she walked forward. "I like that," she said in a coy voice. "Sis, what do you think? Should we turn our brother's new girl in front of him? I would like that." As she looks at me with glee. "Oh, Quinn would be destroyed to see that you moved on."

"Sarah, you know why I am here. Let's do this, and then you can get back to your fun."

Sarah looked back at her older sister with a pouty look. "Ugh, fine. Sorry, cutie, you heard her. No time for fun, all business I guess."

"I am going to wipe that smile off your face," she said as she looked at Sarah.

You could see change in both of my demonic sisters. "You will regret that," Sarah screeched and rushed at Annie with a flash, shoving her against the wall, hard. Annie threw a hard knee to her stomach, but it did not even budge her.

Sarah's hands grabbed her around the throat and began to strangle her.

"Stop it," I yelled, "or I will kill you I swear."

But all of a sudden, Amanda appeared in front of me and startled me, and with a wicked smile, she pulled out a dagger from her sleeve. My eyes widened at the sight of it. My eyes met hers. She walked up and hugged me.

"I know this won't kill you but will make me feel better for you not joining us, brother."

Then my body shook in pain as she jammed the dagger into my side. I yelled out as she dug it deeper. Blood flooded from the wound, but as Amanda went to pull away, I threw my head forward, crashing into hers, sending her stumbling backward clutching her head.

Her pale skin around her eye turned red. "Ugh, how dare you hurt me," she growled. But as she went to step forward toward me, I heard Annie yell, and a white light flash and a small blast of light so bright my eyes hurt sent Sarah flying into her counterpart. Both sprawled against the ground and looked surprised from what just happened. I looked over to Annie. She hunched over. Her neck was red, and she was gasping for air. I looked over in surprise at my sisters, and Sarah was badly burned from the elbow to her hands. She was growling in pain. Amanda looked down at her hurt sister. She looked over to me and smiled. "I am done playing around!" Her eyes started to turn black. The shadows of the rooms seem to flow over Annie, constricting her. The shadows seemed to be an extinction of her body. No matter how hard she struggled, she couldn't break the bondage. Both my sisters walked forward to their victim.

"Please don't!" I struggled against my chains, but they would not break. "Don't do it!"

"Don't do what?" Amanda snapped. "You're going to die one day, but I am going to have fun with this one." Amanda laughed as she looked down at Annie. "How completely helpless. You know what? You're coming with us, girl! And in that moment, the black mist consumed all three of them, and all I heard was Annie's screams as I hung there, helpless.

CHAPTER 5

My body hurt. Seconds ticked away as I hung here, eyes closed, replaying my living nightmare.

"Damn," I growled. My body tensed as I roared and tears flowed without restraint. I had lost my home, my family, and now the girl who saved my life. The pain of the last few days became unbearable, and everything fell into darkness.

In the world of dreams, I returned to a memory before the horror of recent events: the girls playing in the meadows, mother watching over them in the meadows while father trained me, Chris, and Jason. Terry cloud watching. Memories are what make the next day worth seeing. Next thing I know, I was in a field outside the city, the wheat blowing against my hands, the whisper of one hundred familiar voices called out to me to come home. My family was waving at me from the wall. I reached out to them desperately to be next to them to feel a part of a puzzle that is unwhole without me, but I turned around, a whisper in the wind calling to be strong, to not give in. *Is it Annie's voice? Why does it sound so sad?*

The wind carried it like a cold message. I began to follow it, and the closer I got to the forest, the voice became louder until I spotted where it's coming from. My heart stopped as the two girls, Quinn and Annie, battered and bruised, were nailed to a twisted tree. The sight made my body stiff as their wreaked bodies jerked in unnatural motions, but when she spotted me, she stopped, and blood ran from both of their eyes and their mouth turned into a jagged smile and in a hollow voice, moaned, one saying, "You didn't save me" and then the next echoed it.

"Don't let me suffer, not like this," I tried to speak, but nothing came out. Quinn looked at me with pure desperation. My heart broke and I tried to reach her, but before I could grab her, their bodies burst into crows and were gone. I stood there, hands reaching out against the tree where she was, and I looked back at the place I love and the people yelling for me to come back but as I looked up at the tree, I knew it's too late for that now.

There was no going back for any of us, and I turned and walked into the darkness of the woods. But behind me, those who were happy and the sun glowing in their faces had turned into the afflicted. Their smiles turned into snarls. The voices became howls, and the walls full of hanging bodies, the estate burning into flames.

Under my breath, I whispered, "I have chosen the path of death." The dark shroud enveloped me again. My eyes opened to see two soldiers working on the shackles that have bound me. My body was numb, and I didn't even feel my body hit the rough ground. Everything was a blur as the two soldiers dragged my body out, and into the early morning, my eyes focused to see I dragged out into the middle of a row of lit torches. Soldiers lined up in rows, facing a platform. The soldiers jerked me up to my weak legs that shook under my weight.

My vision returned when I saw two soldiers kneeling before the young prince whose face seemed dark with rage, a long black cape shrouding his body. "You two dishonored us all. You men not only left your post, and in this act, my wife was kidnapped in the process! The woman who was chosen by the prophets to be your queen is in the hands of the enemy."

My mind was struggling to put all the pieces together. How did they know what happened?

"You two shall die," the prince said in a grim tone, "but I shall offer you salvation from your failure." He walked up between the two and rested his hands on both men's shoulders. "Fight me, and if you kill me, you shall be set free or die by my hands and regain your honor. Unless you are cowards, fall upon these blades." And threw them to the ground in front of them.

The two men stared at them before looking up at their prince. The man to the right stood up and bowed deeply before speaking. "My prince, I failed you not by my own doing. I was not myself, but I cannot fight you."

And before I knew it, the man took the blade before him and pierced himself through the abdomen and fell to his knees. He didn't cry out even though you could see his body trembling. Nikolai put his hand on the man's head and with the other, drew his blade and with grace, severed the honorable soldier's head from his shoulders. Blood spurted from the wound, and he slumped to the ground.

The man to the left stared at his fallen comrade, took a deep breath, grabbed the blade, and stood before the prince, raised the blade, and the prince smirked and turned his back on him. The soldier roared and charged at him. The blade ripped through the cloak, and just before he had a chance to think of victory, the prince knelt down and lunged up and grabbed the soldier's face with both hands, and the man shrieked in agony as a glow came from his gauntlets. The man's face seemed to have steam coming from his eyes.

My body tensed at the sight. So many things I have learned, and what has seemed like minutes was over in seconds. The man lying before the prince was dead. Nikolai grabbed his cloak and put it back on and stared out among his men. Felix walked up beside him and handed him his sword. "Listen now, men, to me very clearly. Annie, your queen to be, and my wife, is top priority and needs to be recovered swiftly. Any failure will be met with death by the enemy's hand or my own. You men are proud and worthy fighting by my side."

The men roared and raised their weapons, and the men started falling out of order to return to their squads, but I stood there and noticed Felix grabbing the prince and helping him stand. But as I studied him, I noticed his eyes were locked with mine. "William," he snapped, "to my tent now." And he walked away. The two men escorting me pushed me forward through the camp. The men stared at me and whispered as I went past. My strength seemed to be returning to me, but my hunger was unimaginable.

We made our way through the camp and up to a tent much larger than the others. Two men who were known to me as dark knights stood like fortresses, but when I approached, Felix opened the tent and gestured us in. The old knight seemed heavy with grief. I pushed past him, and inside was a large fire with a boar roasting. Men stood around the fire. The prince on the other side was sitting in an elevated chair, his cloak covering his body. I pushed forward toward the men until I told to stop, everyone watching me and ready for any move I might make.

Felix walked up beside me and grabbed my shoulder. "I would say I am sorry how you've been treated, but you must understand our position with recent events."

I looked up at the knight. "How did you know Annie was gone?"

Grim covered all the men's faces. One of the other men stepped forward. He was bald with a long beard that ran along his breathing plate. He looked like he had seen man's battles with scars on his face. "There was a body outside of the camp. One of our men went missing, and we found him nailed to a tree with a grim message caved into the body, stating they have her."

I could see Felix tensing up at the thought of it. My mind drifted off to the glowing of prince's gauntlets. My land on them until I can't hold back the question.

"What was that magic?" I asked Nikolia.

The prince grinned and leaned forward. "Did you think Annie was the only person who can use magic?" He studied my face and leaned back. "I am not gifted like my wife who is truly special. All magic takes a great toll on those who wield this power. If not used, though an object to channel which does weaken, the spell it channels through the body which can be very powerful as well as deadly. You can be drained to the point of helpless exhaustion, burned badly, or even worse, aged years, depending how much you out into it. I see that kind of power can change the world." The proud prince stood up and clutched his fist. "Strength rules our lands, and showing the men and you where I stand is at the top of the ladder." His eyes glowed with authority and pride as if daring me to challenge him. "I saw Annie ran to you earlier," he said as he walked toward me until we were eye-to-eye. "Do not think her kindness is love. I told her to find and survey the land and report back and she brought you here. Your ability to assist me is limited, and your brother is under my care. Do remember he will die without my aid, so I suggest if you are feeling any way toward her, cast it away or your brother dies."

My eyes dropped, not in cowardice, but for the love of my brother. "I do not test him. Yet." The prince returned to his seat with more confidence. He had me under his thumb. I gritted my teeth, but I did not show it. "We are going back, William," the prince said.

My eyes widened. "To the estate?" I whispered.

"Yes, I need a clue on where to find her. She is not only my wife, but the only one who we know can wield the relics that are these stones. If I don't return with this power, the pride lands can erupt into another war. As I stated, power rules our world."

A man in a red robe stepped forward and cleared his voice so that all take notice. His voice was clear and young in comparison to the others. "Young William, I am Victor. I am scribe. I know the talk of war and power is an intoxicating stimulate for you men, but the reality is this. This land is tainted with something none of us has seen before outside of tales in book since before the great war other than the four that was there. Young William, can you tell us what happened to Master Annie. You see, I am her uncle. Annie, as you already noticed, is special, gifted in the magic far beyond her age and past the time where magic was far more powerful. But besides being powerful, she is rash and headstrong. Felix was her guardian since she was a child, but it seems with time, you are not as vigilant as in your youth. the slight does no sit well with the knight as he roars, I

"What are you implying?" The large knight lunged forward, grabbing Victor by his neck as if he weighs nothing. The other men in the tent grabbed the hilts of their blades, but Nikolia tells when the men to stop.

Felix looked around with a fierce glare in his eye, daring someone to interfere before looking at the scribe, gritting his teeth. "Never before have I failed your family! Annie is like the daughter I never had," he bit out. "I will find her even if have to carve a trail of blood through this cursed land. But if I should fail, I will come find you before I die." He left the statement open for Victor's mind to play with before continuing. "You claim to care for her, but against my pleas, you convinced the heads of the family to bring her here."

The man squirmed as he was being choked in the air. "Release me, fool," he squeaked before Felix released his grasp and the man hit the ground with a thud. He grabbed his throat and inhaled deep to regain his composure. Slowly standing up, he put his hood over his head, shadowing his face.

"Felix, you best find her, or maybe your place in this world will fade as will you." The man turned to me. "William, do not let what is inside of you turn you into a beast like some of the men in this room." He turned and a few men followed him out of the tent into the early morning. I breathed deep as the thickness of the air is enough to make your hair stand.

The knight approached the prince and knelt down before him. Nikolia smirked and told Felix to rise. "You have done nothing to upset me." Honestly, he needed to be up into check every once in a while.

"William, listen carefully," the princes said. "Every village we passed so far has been the same story: burned and the villagers missing. We have been at this camp for some time since it's in a good location to scout from. But I am out of patience, and our situation is worsening as each day passes. The last event happened a few days ago, so we are heading back to your estate."

The words hit me deep. The dreams returned and the thought of returning to that nightmare was frightful, each monster and family member with twisted grins howling for me to come home. Then there was the beast behind them, all the wolfish creature.

I looked down at my hands as they shook. I gritted my teeth and summoned my courage and rose. "I understand."

"Straightforward answer, I see. I like that. Now go with these men. They will take you to your brother."

"Jason is okay?"

"Well, he was treated far better than you, and Iyana was taking care of him, so all I know is he is awake."

I turned and rushed out of the tent, my escorts on my heels as I ran through the camp, the men directing me as best as they could. I continued to run toward the tent I was told to go to. Dreams of me, Jason, Felix, and the others, returning my family back to normal flooded my mind. I burst through the tent door and saw him lying on a cot, wrapped in heavy blanket.

I walked up to him and knelt beside him. "Brother, you still alive?"

Half of his face was wrapped in bandages. His eye opened and stared at me. "You're alive, little brother. Is this a dream?" His left arm came out from under the blanket, and he looked frail.

I grasped his hand and told him, "I am alive, but so much has happened. We are returning home to find Annie."

Jason wheezed and said, "Good luck then, brother," as his hand rubbed my face.

"What do you mean? You will be coming with us, won't you?"

He smiled weakly. "No, I won't, brother." His words broke my heart, but when he stood up, horror shrouded over me. His right arm was gone, and when his bandage came off, his eye was gone.

I tried to speak, but all I could do was stare.

"Not as handsome as I used to be, huh? Chris did a number on me when he slammed me against the rock. And the arm was broken into pieces, but infection spread so fast they had to take it to save me. My early thoughts were blown away like a dream. "So, brother, leave me be to rest." His hand was rubbing through my hair.

Tears rolling down my face, I couldn't even speak.

"My battle is over, brother. Do not be sad for me."

I looked back up at him. My brother was smiling as he grabbed the back on my neck and rested his forehead against mine. "My nightmare is over, and I shall awake soon from this dream. But you have to bear both of our burdens now and face our family."

Jason breathed deep and lay down. "Now leave me, brother."

I stood and tried to think of something comforting, but nothing came to mind. "I love you," I said and walked away. When the sun hit my face, my world spun, but I stood tall even though the weight of this is heavy on my soul. I ran my hand over my face and breathed deeply.

"Hey, boy," I heard from nearby. I looked over and saw a short stocky man. "Yes, you," he barked. "Come with me."

I walked over and looked down and studied him. Shorter like Annie but his arms were massive. "You must be a blacksmith, I presume."

"Hmm, well, seems you are not as dumb as you look, William."

"Thank you, I guess," I said with uncertainty.

"Oh I jest, boy, now come. I have some gifts for you that are worth your weight in gold."

My interest piqued as I followed the dwarfed man. Soon, we arrived to a cart where he opened the back to find so many shiny breastplates to exotic helmets and greaves. Blades of all shapes and design. My mind ran wild at the thought. "Can I?" I asked the man.

He bellowed in laughter. "Yes, my boy. But you still haven't asked me my name." My face became red with embarrassment. I took a step back. Before I could ask, he bellowed. "I am the Famous Hagvar." He gleamed with pride.

"Hmm, I never heard of you," I said without thinking.

His pride turned to anger. "Of course no, you fool. You are not from our land." And he kicked me in the leg. I winced in pain as I grasped my knee. "Sorry," I tried and bit out as a few nearby soldiers laughed at the spectacle. "Sorry, sorry," I said before the mad dwarf could kick me again.

"Your luck, boy. Not wise to disrespect a blacksmith. As you see, my craft is art. Go see for yourself. Choose what you want."

I looked around and found a breastplate that has a wolf as a sigil engraved into it. It's a little big, but I tightened up the straps until it's snug, as well as some leggings and forearm wraps. The feel of too much armor made me feel slow. Plus I know the monster inside was still there, but it's been quiet.

"You look good, boy. I turned you into a proper soldier. Now all you need is a blade." The dwarf ran his hand over his chin and walked back around the cart and returned with a sword that looked like Felix's. "It's kinda heavy with a ruby in the cross block."

"It's beautiful," I told Hagvar.

He pounded his chest and said, "See, I knew the boy would like it. Now just don't die fast enough to give that blade a good test."

I studied the blade and thought of what I have to do when we heard a loud horn go off. *Burrhhhhh,* it blasted again. Soldiers started rushing into formations.

"Huh? What do I do?" I asked Hagvar.

"Go find Felix. Seems like it's time to leave."

I turned and spotted the knight walking toward a group of soldiers. I rushed up to the knight, and before I could speak, he looked down at me and actually cracked a smile. "Look at you, William, not half bad. But there is no time for small talk. We are leaving back toward the estate. Prepare yourself."

My head dropped as all I could say is Jason's name. "Don't worry for him. He will be coming too. In the center is the medical teams. I am sorry for what happened to him. But our battle has just begun. Look around you, William. There are a few hundred men here ready to face this with you. Me, Nikolia, Iyana, and even Victor is coming as well, though personally, I hope he doesn't make it. Together then, we go to whatever end waits for us." He grabbed my shoulder and we fell in line. Nikolia stood on a plate form with his personal guard, watching as the men filed out of the camp toward my home. Some march for glory and fame, some for honor. I marched for my family, either to save them or save them from themselves.

"Annie, I hope you're still alive." But deep down, I know she is too strong to die so easily. I don't know if I have the strength to do what I have to but I knew I must try.

CHAPTER 6

The morning sun was quickly swallowed by dark rain clouds. The heavens screamed and boomed with fierce lightning that made the ground tremble. The trees took on a haunting form in the flashes of bright white light. But we marched on. Only a few days away from home.

Each step felt like we were walking to our deaths, but we marched on. The storm raged all day until we got signal to stop. My body ached from wearing this armor and excited to rest my body. Men started setting up tents and torches around the perimeter. It's a large camp with about thirty to forty tents. I found Felix as the men set up their areas and got guard shifts set up for the night.

The tall knight approached me. In the flashing light, he looked quite terrifying. "Damn, rain needs to stop," he grumbled. "I dislike omens like this."

"Omens? What do you mean?"

"It's just a feeling," he explained and pointed into a nearby tent, and we headed inside. A few men were already inside, setting up a fire. "Ah, nights like these really make me feel my age," he scoffed. A few laughed at the joke as the fire burned bright. I stared into the flames and listened to the men tell tales of Felix's bravery or how they all got out of grim situations. They passed some jerky around, and I scoffed it down quickly. Ugh, I forgot how good food tasted. It's been a minute since my last meal.

Soon the questions moved to me and what they were in store for with my family. Their faces did not convey confidence as myself, and Felix told our tale.

"Demons," one man called out, "they cannot be killed."

But Felix waved his fears off. "I battle strongest of them, and I have stood toe to toe. But if you are not the soldiers I thought you all are, then stay out of my way and let a real soldier show you the way."

The men stared at one another and turned to Felix and told him that they will be by his side till the end.

"How about you, William?"

The question caught me off guard. "What do you mean?" I asked, puzzled.

"To face your family and more so, your brother."

I simply nodded my head and calmly said there was no going back now.

"Well, isn't the most inspiring speech I ever heard," one of the men joked, but Felix shot him a look that put the man in his place.

"You will soon know what it's like, so eat, Hardy, and try and sleep, men, because soon we go to war."

We all lay down, and I slipped deep into my dreams. It all seemed foggy. I couldn't see where I was at, but it looked like a hall. I walked forward and saw a large human-sized crystal. I heard hisses of my sister's but I couldn't see them. Terry's voice was telling someone they couldn't hide in there forever. The voices swirled around as they taunted, but it didn't seem like they were aimed toward me. I moved toward the crystal and saw something inside of it; I was frozen. My breath became ragged as I approach it and realized it's Annie. I put my hands on its surface, and her eyes opened. Annie and Quinn were embracing.

I yelled and tried to break inside to get them. Our eyes met, and I could hear her voice inside of my head. "Come home and save me." She continued that she couldn't hold this forever. Annie's voice faded away as her eyes closed. Their bodies were frozen away inside this spell waiting for us. I reached out and put my hand against the crystal. "I will come for you two, I promise," I growled.

The air grew thick as my hair stood up. I looked past Annie and noticed in the shadow a large man stirring. Then I noticed the axe next to him which made me grab for my blade at my side, but when I reached for my hilt, there was nothing there. His eyes cracked open slowly, and red glow filled the darkness around him. The man breathed in deep and exhaled with a deep growl. Our eyes locked, but I couldn't tell if he could actually see me. His hands moved slowly as if he had been in a long slumber.

But in a flash, the monster of a man hurled his axe my way, but by body refused to listen to me as if I had lost all control. I went to yell as the axe hit me, but instead of ripping into my flesh, it went right through me and barreled into a pillar, smashing it into pieces with a loud boom. I looked behind me and saw the axe stuck into wall. My body shook at the ferocity of the act. I looked back at my brother. The man had stood up and walked within a few feet of me. I stared up at him and wished it was really him. He stopped before me as my sisters came from the shadows and wrapped around Chris. Their faces were twisted as they hissed at me. I wanted to cry, but I remembered what happened to Jason.

"They can't see you, but we can feel your presence, brother." A slim man walked out. It's Terry. He looked more pale than before.

Anger flowed through my blood like fire, but as I went to roar back, the crystal glowed bright, and in an intense flash, I cracked open my eyes and the hall shadows faded away. My sisters were beautiful and smiling, not with wicked jagged smiles. My brother returned to human state. He looked down at his body and looked at me. "Brother, I am sorry," he said.

The man before me had never once apologized to me. The rage in my body evaporated like the passing wind.

"Brother," the girls called out. "Do not despair. We don't have long but we love you."

The words broke me down as tears flowed down my face. "I don't want to fight you," I choked out.

My brother smiled and rested his hand on my shoulder. "Little brother, you have to be the one who saves us from this curse. For what we have become is not for this world. If you don't stop it with her"—he nodded to Annie—"this world will fall to the affliction that has been awoken."

"Brother, I don't know if I can, but I will try."

He smiled and tried to say something but fell to his knees. He grabbed his throat, and my sisters screamed as if they were being attacked by something we couldn't see. Chris's body rippled in dark veins as his hair fell out. My sisters' bodied twisted in unnatural ways, and horror spread over my body.

I looked over, and Terry was chanting something and was as pale as before. "Terry, stop!" I yelled. "What are you doing?"

He paid no attention to my pleas. The shadows grew and moved toward us. Their screams became deafening, but as I reached out to save them, I was jerked awake by screams and horns blowing.

Felix jumped up, grabbed his blade, yelled for us to "get up! Prepare yourselves. We are under attack."

Then the men and I roared as we rushed outside into the fray. The rain was coming down as we saw the ghouls of different sizes rushing from the darkness into the camp and clashing with the men. Bodies of our comrades and monsters were engaged in fierce combat. Roars and screams filled my ears that threatened to overwhelm me.

I peered into the darkness as lightning relieved darkness the woods, harboring large numbers of monsters that threatened to swallow us alive. Men rushed from the tents and fought for their lives. I pushed forward with Felix into the next tent, and when we opened it, a man was reaching up to us as a beast ripped into his flesh. The sight took me back as the beast turned and snarled, showing bits of flesh in its jaws. Its body tensed and threatened to lung for us, but before it could lung at me, Felix swung his blade and cut the beast down. The monster fell hard to the ground and shook violently as life left its body.

I rushed forward and grabbed the man's hand. He looked so confused and went limp. Moments later, his eyes filled with fear. I looked back at the knight, and he shook his head, knowing there was no more we could do. We hardened our courage and left the dead man and headed back out into the battle. As I came out of the tent, a man was running up to us. His helmet had claw marks over it. He was too far away when he tried to yell something out, but the storm and roars of the battle drowned him out, but as he went to say it again, a large half-breed smashed into the soldier, knocking him down, and started mauling him.

I reacted quickly and leaped forward and with my new blade, swung down and cut the beast's head in two. Blood covered the soldier as he laughed nervously. I reach down to help him up to his feet.

"Thank you so much. I thought I was done for." But as I went to say something, he talked over me. "We have to get to the prince. A large number have broken through and seemed to be heading there," he told me.

I nodded to him and wished him luck. I looked back at the knight's direction where four monsters had attacked him. He had one monster in a headlock as he stabbed another through the chest, turning his blade red. Another rushed toward him but was met with the creatures he was holding, and they crashed into a tent, knocking it down. The last monster was large and stood tall roaring at Felix and made charges at him. He looked ready to meet it head on. As the beast lunged, Felix grabbed a nearby shield and raised it just in time and leaned all his might into it. The crash was so hard you could hear its bones break as the knight didn't budge an inch; and the beast fell to the ground, and you could hear its ragged breathing as it fell still.

The man looked up to the heavens, roared for the men to fight for their honor and their lives. Men roared back in encouragement. I moved to Felix. I told him what the soldier has said. "I see then. Let's go. It seems the battle is dying down over here."

We started heading for the center of the camp. I passed a tent. Something caught my attention as a man in robe walked quickly passed. Felix didn't see me stop as he continued to head to where his prince was. I tried to follow, but my body was telling me to go forward. So I pressed forward slowly. Bodies littered the narrow gaps between the tents, some covered in blood and ripped marks. The sight was nerve-racking. But as I continued, I came behind the cloaked figure. "Who are you?" I yelled. When the figure turned and the robe fells it's him—the one who started it all.

The wolfish man stood before as my heart pounded against my chest. "It's you," I roared and raised my weapon.

He smiled. "Can you feel it, boy?" as he raised his hand up to me. "My gift spreads through and around this camp as we speak. I wish your family could see this, but it seems like the girl is more trouble than I expected. So I come to do this myself. You will join me, boy. You don't have a choice."

"Go to hell," I roared and rushed forward. "Give them back, you bastard," as I brought my blade down to the man who took it all from me.

The world slowed down as my eyes locked with him. I could see the raindrops around me as if everything was in slow motion. But in a flash, he seemed to disappear, and my blade struck the ground. I looked around to see where he had gone. But as I turned my head, I came inches from the face of my nightmares. His fierce eyes pierced through mine. And his teeth showed.

"I did not come to fight you like this," as his fist slammed into my breastplate, cracking it where his fist connected. The force of the blow slammed me into the ground. He stood over me and roared. "Now show me, my child, my gift."

My rage boiled as it seemed like the difference in our strength was too great. I dropped my blade and punched the ground and roared. My body jolted with agony. My arms' bones cracked and snapped as it grew longer. The skin darkened and red veins burst from the flesh. The pain was unreal. My nails grew until they were almost bladelike. But it seemed different this time. My face felt different. My teeth felt like they were razor-sharp. My senses felt heightened. But when I looked down into the pool of water, the lightning let me see what I was slowly becoming. My right eye was bright yellow and the teeth in my mouth looked animalistic. Rage consumed and I crouched, launched myself through the air, power I never felt before.

The beast himself was caught off guard, and I smashed my fist into the chest of the monster. But this time, it blew him back into a few boxes. He grunted and looked up just in time to see me leaping in the air. His eyes that were filled with certainty now seemed to have all too human qualities.

"Die," I roared as I threw everything I had into the next hit that connected with his face. I could feel his bones cracking with the blow. But as soon as I hit him, I felt his foot come up and slam into my stomach, throwing me off into the blood-soaked earth. I gasped for air, got up to one knee. I looked up to see the wolfish man standing up, blood coming from his mouth.

"It seemed my gift had indeed made you powerful, boy. But as you can tell, each time you use it, you become more beast than man. So how many times before it consumes you?"

I breathed deep and regained my composure. "What are you?"

He looked at me through the darkness. "I am Sin, the lord of the lost and reaper of this world. I was summoned long ago, but I was dormant for longer than I can remember. But I was awoken, and your village and others were sacrificed as a pact to gain power. Now this county shall fall and the others with it."

But before he could continue, my body twisted in pain, and I started to shake violently as my body started to turn back into its normal form. As I roared in pain, I could hear him taunting me. "So that's it, huh? Can't hold it for very long. Don't worry. Soon it will consume you and your eternal slumber will start and the monster will own your body."

I clawed at the ground as it completed its cycle. I heard voices other than our own, but my vision cut in and out, just brief glimpses of horror. Five soldiers rushed in and engaged Sin and all I could hear are their screams. I could hear bodies and blades hitting the ground as the fight continued. I could hear one soldier groaning in a way that haunted and I saw him holding his guts. A body slammed against me, and I was lying face-to-face with a twisted face of man in his last moments. He tried to speak, but blood burst from his mouth onto my face. My body shook as I stood up, and all I could hear was a bone-chilling whisper. "I will be watching."

I looked around and saw the men that were fighting him now lying dead around me. I stood up and grabbed my blade that was covered in gore. I stumbled to where I last saw Felix going. Bodies littered the ground, monsters and men alike. I tried to keep walking forward when I felt a hand grab me and I fell into few bodies.

"Help," I heard in a ragged voice. I looked down and saw the dwarf-sized man named Hagvar. I crawled over to him, and I saw the wound he's trying to stop bleeding. I grabbed his hand and he looked at me with fear. "Young William, what have you done to my armor?"

I looked down and saw it cracked where Sin's fist struck me. "I am sorry," I tried to say but it fell short. Because before I could say it, he died and fell still. My shoulders felt so heavy as I closed his eyes and stood up. I looked down back at the proud blacksmith and pushed forward. I could still hear some fighting going on, but all I saw were some scared soldiers holding their fallen comrades or tending to the wounded. I finally made it to the center to see bodies of beasts and men surrounding Nikolia and Felix. The knights in black armor were standing guard and noticed me walking up.

They looked battered and exhausted. Nikolia saw me and stood. "Well, out of all the people who have died today, you survived, huh? Seems like you're not as weak as I thought."

I sneered at him and saw Felix. He looked distant, but when he saw me, he stood and approached me. "Where did you go? It was bad here. So many have died but it seems you live on. I think the God's favor is on you."

"No, I think they pity me to let me suffer in this land," I said without thinking.

The knight looked around. "We all have a job to do, William. Stay focused." And he grasped my shoulder and headed over to a soldier walking from behind a tent. They spoke for a moment, and Felix looked back at the prince. "The enemy is retreating. It seems we have pushed them back. Good." He stood up and thrust his blade into the air.

Soldiers, battered and bruised, gathered around. "We have won." And the men roared in excitement. "But it is not over. Your brothers who have fallen here tonight will be remembered by you who survived. Their tales of glory will be sung and told to their loved ones, and we all shall push forward and will not stop until we die or save our kingdom. If we fail here, the consequences will be felt, my brothers. So harden your hearts and let's get the job done."

The men roared and fell out to help the wounded and find the ones they cared about.

The storm faded away, and I found myself sitting around a fire with Felix and the prince. I stared deep into the flames, and I couldn't pull my eyes away. "I saw him," I said out loud but to no one in particular.

Nikolai didn't even look as he sharpened his blade. "Who do you speak of?" he asked finally.

My heartbeat pounded as I recalled the moments between us. "Sin, his name is Sin." He finally looked toward me. "The creature who started it all, the monster who took my family."

Felix looked my way. "Yeah, was here during the battle?" he asked, puzzled.

"Yeah, I fought him after we got split up and almost didn't make, it but it seems he spared me once more. He told me he was summoned, I guess by someone who desired power and was willing to sacrifice this land to obtain it. But now he is awake and is hell-bent on spreading his gift."

Soldiers stirred around us that overheard me. Some continued to conduct their tasks, clearing bodies and burning the monsters.

"Gift, huh?" Nikolai said with a snarl. "I will gift him death that none has experienced with my bare hands when I find my wife."

Felix stood and looked down at us. "We lost a lot of good men. Around fifty were dead and plenty were wounded. We must choose our battles wisely because men's power is our lifeline here, and with no one coming to our aid, let's hope there are a few villages that stand still that can assist us."

The prince growled, "Do you not think we have the men to head to the estate?"

"Of course I do not say that, my prince. I am only saying we should move now before our enemy can attack or search for some assistance."

"No," the prince bit out, "we move out as soon as possible." The prince looked at Felix. "Summon the company leaders and tell them to forget the dead. We move now."

"Your will is my hand," and turned to his orders.

I breathed deep. No rest for the weary I suppose.

Nikolai shot a piercing glance and growled, "Only the dead rest here."

The morning blurred by as the men readied themselves. Some congregated for prayer then got a quick bite to eat and move into their formation. Iyana approached me, but her eyes looked distant. "Hey, I would ask how have you been, but I could only imagine." She ran a stained bloody hand through her hair but managed to crack a smile.

I had been in many bad situations, but after all this, I am going to request to leave to go rest somewhere quiet. I tried to think of a place like that but nothing comes to mind. "So, ugh, was there something you needed?"

"Oh yeah, so the wounded are heading back to the fort we established. Jason and the rest of us will be heading back since we would only be a burden now. They can't spare any men, so we are on our own. Your brother told me to tell you he will be watching."

The words that should bring comfort only reminded me of that monster. The words sent shivers up my spine. But I cracked a smile. "Tell him to rest and I will come back soon."

She nodded and turned away. I looked forward as the survivors and battle-able men headed off in two separate directions. I started to notice familiar areas from a past that seemed so long ago. I walked beside men that were cheering days ago for battle, but now, some men's faces looked dark and hollow. But there was no turning back for us anymore.

It's nearly midday when we marched past a familiar valley. It's where we battled my brother. I could see rotten corpses of ghouls and blasted area where Annie showed us what true power was. I could relive each emotion as I replayed the battle in my mind. I wanted to approach Felix and talk to him about it, but he was somewhere near the front of the column. We continued on but each step closer, my stomach felt like it's twisted. I could taste blood in my mouth as my mind raced like something bad had happened. But before I know it, the sun was starting to fall from the sky as the day was coming to a close. The formation stopped, and I walked to the front. We were at the edge of the woods, not too far down the mountain that over-looked the village where we met Felix and Annie.

Nikolai ordered the men to set up campfires and send out patrols to keep us from being snuck up on. But I had a feeling they were waiting for us to make our move. The moon rose above us, and it's full tonight. I stared up at it as the men ate their meals and rested. A shadow came up from behind me that spooked me, but as I went to draw my blade, I saw it's Felix who laughed lightly at my reaction. "William, let's go."

"Where?" I asked.

He looked down at me and lit a torch. "Where it all began."

Each step it felt like we were rewinding time. It'd been such a short amount of time, but I felt like in that time, I had aged a few years. We slowly made our way up the mountain overlooking my old home, not a word said between us until we arrive. In my mind, I replayed each moment as if I was living it all over again.

The old knight walked a few paces and stared at the building down below us. "Seems quiet. You think they are there?" I asked the old knight.

He rubbed his hand through his hair and looked down toward me. "William, we have been through a lot together, as well having lost people we have been close to. I would gladly fight by your side any day and call you brother," he said as he held his hand out to me.

I couldn't help it even through all this despair. I smiled and grasped his forearm. As the moment passed, we looked down to our next battle. I laughed a little to myself which took the knight off guard. "What are you laughing about? Has madness already taken root in your mind," he said, shoving me slightly.

"No, no. I was just thinking, if I save the princess and Nikolia, maybe I can steal a kiss and piss him off?"

Felix managed to crack a smile. "You read too many hero stories."

I looked up into the night sky and breathed deep and slowly exhaled. "Yeah, you're probably right."

The chill of the wind blew past when we heard a branch snap behind us. Me and Felix drew our blades and swung around. We could hear it coming closer each moment. My heart started to race as Felix stretched his arm out with the torch to hopefully see who or what it was before it's already on us.

But slowly, a shadow moved closer to us before falling down. Felix moved closer in a low voice, telling me hurry over. I saw a man who was gravely wounded. It's a soldier who returned with the other caravan back to the fort. He looked ghostly as he grasped up at Felix. "My lord," he stuttered out, his eyes searching frantically. "The woods came alive. The shadows came alive and started killing the men before the howls came and the monsters slaughtered many of us." He choked and blood started to come from his mouth before convulsing violently and died in the old knight's arms.

I am struck with grief, knowing this was my sisters' doing. "Damn," I growled. My mind drifted to Jason, but I stopped myself so I don't crumble.

"You did a brave thing telling us this, soldier." He closed his eyes. "Now be free and join your brothers in the afterlife and know no pain." He gently laid the man's head down and started walking back toward the camp.

I took one more glance at the soldier and turned to follow Felix into the night. We swiftly returned back to camp. We ran into a patrol of soldiers; one of the men rushed to us.

"Something is wrong, Felix. Do you feel that and hear that noise?" I didn't notice it until the man pointed it out, but now my body grew tense. Felix nodded and pushed past the men and ran off toward camp with me at his heels.

Soon we were rushing into the camp, but as we passed clusters of men who looked on edge, some had their weapons ready. We approached the prince's tent. There were three black knights who had their weapons drawn and standing off with a few captains. Felix and I brushed past them.

Felix roared, "What in the hell is the meaning of this?"

I stood near Felix and kept my guard up in case someone makes a move.

The head, Nikolai's personal guard, stepped forward and slowly removed their helmet. My eyes widened since not only have I never heard one of them speak, let alone seen their faces. But as the helmet fell, I saw the face of a young woman with raven black hair. Her skin was flawless and her eyes were like daggers. She looked around at the men until her eyes met Felix's. "You approach your prince's tent in the means of getting past me. You shall fall before me." As she spoke, a blast of wind that looked black came from the tent door and a glimpse of Nikolia; his eyes were black, and he was gripping at his hair, growling as if something was attacking his body.

I looked up at Felix. "We must get past them. Something is wrong."

But the female overheard me and pointed her blade at me. "You, young man, would step up to me."

I looked back at the woman. "Nikolai could be dying in there," I said as I gestured behind her.

Her eyes closed and breathed deep, her hair whipping in the unnatural wind. "My orders. Stand, young man. To the death and beyond my life is at my prince's whims. I was ordered to not let anyone pass, and I will die by that order."

I growled deep. "You know, being on the same side, we should not be fighting. I don't know if any of you thought about this, but we are in front of a place that could be the deaths of all of us. And whatever is happening to your prince seems like something we need to figure it out."

The wind whipped around us, but her eyes never left mine. "You are not from our land, outsider. Power rules our way. And fighting is very common between those who desire power and those who cling to it."

"You are all insane," I roared as I drew my blade as well as Felix. The three dark knights raised theirs as well. The men gossiped to themselves but continued to be aware of our position.

But before the battle started, we heard horns blown toward the direction of the estate. The wind died down and everything went silent. Everyone turned and chilled as another dreary blast of a horn echoed. All of a sudden, Victor, in his red robe, came out of the tent and put a hand on the tall female's shoulder. "Thank you for entertaining them. Victor, what have you done?"

Felix growled, drawing his blade up. The scribe pulled down his hood and strange marking covered his face. "This land has been filled with so much magic unlike in the pride lands. I was able to give our prince even more power though the cost is grave and will have to be paid soon."

"Damn you, Victor. You could kill him with things you have no control over. I assured us victory and the retrieval of my niece. Nikolai and I are willing to give it all. Are you willing to die for Felix? If it wasn't for you letting her escape your sight, we would have not even had to do this. Annie is more than a woman. She herself is a weapon. Without the body she can change the balance of power. You're going to use her as a weapon," Felix growled.

"Use her?" Victor laughed. "You fool, I need not explain anything to you."

In the tense moment, Nikolia walked out. The prince's body had noticeably bulked up from before. His eyes were darker than before. Is he more like Chris now? *No, something different,* I thought to myself.

Felix readied the men. "We go to war." Felix didn't move but only looked at his prince. Their stare off his intense but the old knight backed down. I breathed heavily, knowing Felix had went toe to toe with my brother but backed down from him. *How strong is he?* I wondered. The men watching all returned to their formations.

The female knight with long black hair walked up to me and shoved her shoulder into mine. I regained my balance. "What was that for?"

She was slightly taller than me, but we were eye locked. "You were going to fight me. It takes a lot of guts, but since you know not who I am, I shall tell you. I am Siren. Do not die today because I want to test you when you are a real man."

I blushed in anger. "I am a real man, you overgrown woman."

She only smiled and put on her helmet and left with Felix. I found myself alone as the men prepared for battle. I didn't know who was more terrifying: the monster and my family or the power struggle of my supposed comrades. Though I cast the thoughts away quickly, I grabbed cup full of water and drank deep.

A soldier walked up to me and held out his hand. "This world has succumb to madness," he said, grasping his hand and standing up. "Do not let it take you with it."

I looked at the man and nodded. "Best of luck out there" and walked toward my destiny. I pushed through lines of men to the edge of woods and stared into the morning dawn. Soon, the sun would shine on us once more. I looked over to the prince who went under some kind of transformation. The prince walked forward into the field and turned around and looked at us all. He said nothing, but he didn't need to. Another blast of a horn, and I started to notice half-breeds pouring out of the open gate. The prince turned around and charged forward.

Each man summoned a mighty roar of courage, and we all charged along. Each stride, I gripped my blade harder. I could feel my body tense. My fear and pride, my sadness and rage all pulled at me from the inside. The monsters lining up before us charged into us. The battle lines crashed like waves into one another. I roared and saw my first enemy. I threw myself through the air and crashed my shoulder into the beast, plowing it and the one behind it over. I used the momentum to roll over to my feet and stab my blade down into the monster's back then ripped it out, blood covering my blade.

Another monster leaped at me. I spun my blade like a whirl-wind, meeting the monster's face, cleaving through the top part of its head, sending its body crashing past me. The enemies were few out here, but bodies littered the battlefield, the sounds of battle consuming your mind. Me and about twenty men pushed the enemy back on our side until we were in the shadow of the wooden wall. I looked over and saw the other squads moving up to the wall as well. But there were many men dead in the fields.

I focused my mind. Nikolai rushed up to the gate, covered in gore, with Felix by his side. We all nodded at each other and rushed at the gate into the lower part of the town. Charred corpses littered the ground from when we were here last. But as we rushed into the courtyard with the fountain in the center, it's all quiet. As the last man filed through the gate, it slammed shut.

"Spread out," said Nikolia. Then we heard another horn blast. Screeching filled our ears as we saw two figures coming out through an alley way before us. The town became alive with more creatures. I pushed my way to the front of the line.

My sisters were wrapped around the mother's statue, their claws digging into the stone. "Welcome home, brother. Seems like you brought friends," Amanda growled.

Sarah wrapped her arm around her sister. "Worry not, we have our own lovely pets we can let them play with." They started to giggle. "Now die!" they both snarled.

And monsters poured out of the woodworks. Monsters' eyes consumed with madness as hordes of creatures closed the distance.

"Hold the line, men," the prince screamed as men roared as the masses clashed into one another. Men thrust their blades and tore flesh from the bones, filling the air once again with intoxicating sounds of battle. I cut down each abomination before me. But I couldn't draw my eyes away from my sisters, the sight of them filling me with rage.

Charging, I roared, thrusting my blade in their direction. Soon the lines broke, and men struggled for their lives in groups. But in my tunnel, I kept pushing forward through the horror. Each stride before was over another corpse. But then out of the black mass of red eyes and snapping jaws, a large monster blocked my path. I roared, eyes filled with madness, and rammed my blade into the monster. Its teeth snapping at me, I pushed back a step and ripped my blade from his chest and thrust my boot into its body, sending it into the corner of the fountain, cracking its head.

Two soldiers rushed up to my side. One missed his helmet and was badly bleeding from his forehead. The other's eyes were wide, jaw clenched, but I could hear him telling me, "We have your back."

I looked around and saw we had been cut off from the main battle and had been surrounded. But it did not faze me. I looked up at the statue where my siblings were, but seeing an opportunity, they had leaped down, rushed toward me. I saw them; our eyes locked. The world seemed drowned out as I brought my blade up and rushed forward. A clear path had been opened to let the showdown commence. As we were feet from one another, I leaped in the air, blade overhead, trying to cleave her in half, but Amanda burst into a plume of smoke, inches before my blade reached her. My blade hit the ground, flashing sparks as a hand with sharp claws jutted forward through the mist but narrowly missed and cut my cheek.

Her eyes were barely visible. Our bodies collided, but with my mass, my shoulder drove her body hard into the ground with gasp of air rushing out of her chest. I rolled over with the momentum and brought my blade up, just in time to parry the next blade from my sister, sending her sliding back. Both sisters of mine stood before me. My chest was heavy and my limbs shook. My body tensed as I yelled out and rushed forward, but before I closed the distance, they backed away into the crowd of creatures surrounding us. But behind them revealed the two soldiers who were next to me. One was dead on the ground, eyes completely blank of life, his guts being torn into, his blood covering the black flesh of creatures. The other, who had lost his helmet, has wide eyes, staring at me, crawling as two monsters were fighting over his torn-off leg. Blood gushed from the wound, but he still held up his blade to continue fighting. The scene I was witnessing was unreal. The rage had left me as the realization hit me like a ton of bricks. Because of my carelessness, they followed me into this situation and got cut off from the others.

But in that fleeting moment, I felt burning pain from my back. I turned to see Amanda's twisted smile. Then another jolt, I looked down and Sarah's claws buried into my chest. The pain was excruciating, and my brain was blank, out of shock.

Amanda's lips were warm against my ear. "Drink it in, brother." Her hand gripped my hair, making me look at the soldier who was crawling toward me, getting torn to shreds before his screams consumed me. Tears rolled down my face.

"Don't worry, brother. Those two girls will not live long, so die quickly." The thought jolted something deep within me, like a wall that was held up by sheer will had come crashing down. My body convulsed. I grabbed Sarah by the hair and smashed my forehead, watching her eyes roll in the back of her head. I pushed her off, my blood covering her fingers.

Amanda hissed and tried to shove the blade deeper to finish me, but it wouldn't move. My body felt like it's on fire as steam filled my wound and started to jut from my eyes, feeling her blade jolt from and leave my body. I twisted around and swung my blade with my right arm, but as my blade should have hit, she was gone in a mist of black smoke. I came to stop and fell to one knee. A small amount of blood filled my mouth and came from one corner of my mouth. My body shook as I felt a well of rage consume me. I looked up to the sky. "I want you to die," I roar that sounded more beast than man, but inside, I heard another whisper to let me do it. I looked around, watching the horrors of battle unfold around me, blood pouring from grotesque wounds, heads and limps missing. Bodies piled on one another with twisted expressions. I looked up and saw the moon rising into the sky. I grasped up to it and roared, and then in that moment, I let go.

"Kill them all," I heard it say. My body rocked, but this time, I felt no pain as my armor burst from my body. I felt like I had lost control and someone dark had taken possession of me. My hand reaching for the sky twisted and changed, and I started to grow. My roar turned into a deep howl. As then it took over. The battle seemed to stop as my transformation struck fear into all who witnessed the birth of a true horror.

My claws gripped and tore into the earth beneath me. I searched and saw my sisters wrapped around the mother statue. I stepped forward, and my body tensed as I roared so loud. "Half-breed, rush out of my path." My sisters' faces were unsure. My primal rage took over as a wrecking ball. I plowed through the half-breeds and dived into the statue, trying to catch my sisters off guard, but Amanda had just enough time to leap off, grabbing her sister and flashing into smoke, but my instincts were sharp and sensed where she was going to appear, and as she did on the top of a building, I leaped and grasped. As she reappeared, her face of horror as she pushed Sarah out of the way of my claws. I watched her fall almost in slow motion, her face almost looking like they did before. But as my head turned, meeting Amanda, her eyes were wide, her twisted smile gone. Agony rippled through her body as I squeezed tighter. She tried to speak but words never come. She pressed on my paws and dug her nails deep into my flesh. My rage boiled over, and her face turned almost human again, and a single tear ran down her face as I lunged forward with my mouth open.

Her horrible scream filled my ears like a violin sweet music as I ripped into her, her blood filling my mouth like hot wine. When her screams stopped, I lifted her mangled body up and slammed her lifeless body through the roof of the building. I jerked my head to the sky and roared with all the beast's rage, then I heard Sarah's voice "William," from the other side of the roof. I looked down and snarled my bloody teeth at her.

She was holding a blade by her side. "You killed her, you bastard!" She rushed forward, pointing the blade toward my chest.

My vision went blurry as her eyes were glowing brighter like before back in the cell. I roared and swiped my large claws at her, but she dodged it and slammed the blade into my chest. The pain didn't even affect me. I looked down at her with a deep growl as she pushed the blade deeper. Steam started to seep out. Ours eyes locked, then the look I waited for...fear...she let the blade go before it's pushed out and fell to the roof. She started to back away. My eyes looked down at the blade then back up to Sarah.

She was frightened and hissed at me. I roared and grasped for Sarah. She fought frantically, but mis stepped and fell to the ground. I lunged myself at her and slammed into the building next to us as we both hit the ground with a thud. Sarah rushed over and leaped on top of me and ripped into my body with her claws that would shred a man but me. I saw the blood, but I couldn't feel it. I roared and batted her to the side of the building, kicking up dust.

She grunted and lunged back at me, but I caught her and slammed her against a wood post that had a stake sticking out if it. Her face was covered in shock as she grasped the spike. I held her there and roared. Blood gushed as she coughed from her mouth. She grasped my fur but knew it's too late. Soon her body stopped shaking and her face went blank. I looked up to the sky and roared one last time with all my power. The howl turned into hysterical crying as I fell before her.

I held her and sobbed like a child. "Damn you," I cried out. "Damn you." My legs shook as I slowly fell to my knees, holding my sister's foot. I didn't even notice but Felix and few men, the soldiers, drew their blades, but I heard him tell them to stand down. I was limp as his hand fell on my shoulder. I gripped his hand with mine and stood, unable to meet my sister's eyes.

"Come, the battle is not over." I calmed myself and as we moved up the crowded and war-torn streets, bodies littered the streets even more than before when everything happened. We came up to a large crowd of men who had survived. Nikolia, who was looking not so good, he was covered in bite marks. "So that's what you truly are, William."

Siren looked over at me, eyes looking unsure if I was still the same man.

"Let's finish this," was all I managed to say as I stood before group of men.

The prince smiled. "Then let's finish this."

We took time to refit and catch our breath. I felt so numb to everything as if I ripped my own beating heart from my chest. But I reminded myself Quinn is still in there with Annie.

Felix was ahead by the mansion. We were approaching the yard where two bodies lay. I knew one of the men. His head was caved in from my brother's axe. Felix walked next to me. "You know this man?"

"Yes, his name was Gustav. He sacrificed himself to give us time to escape."

The tall knight nodded and continued, "I will make your sacrifice mean something." And he rose up.

Soldiers were trying to open the door, but it seemed stuck. "Oh? Have you tried pulling instead of pushing the door?"

A few men laughed at the jest, but it quickly passed. As we walked up to Felix, the door was almost down. He growled. A few moments passed and the door fell open. We rushed inside. And that first night, when everything happened, came back to me. I didn't dare go upstairs because of memories. Quickly, the building was searched, and one of the men came running back.

There was a staircase leading down. As I approached the stairs, memories flooded back to me where I could almost feel Gustav's hand on my shoulder. Felix and the prince looked back to me. My vision of Annie and Quinn being in a large hall. "She is underground," I stated.

We all approached the staircases. Weapons drawn, we pressed forward. Down the stairs, I retraced my steps, seeing my shadow from days prior. Soon, we turned down a hall and a light of a large hall. We filled in and my heart leaped as I saw Annie's crystal. Both ladies were in each other's arms.

Felix and Nikolia pressed forward when I yelled for them to stop. Two large eyes slowly opened from the darkness. "You kept me waiting so long, brother."

My memory flashed of what happened when he opened his eyes, but I just had enough time to yell "Move" as his monstrous axe cleaved through ten men who were not fast enough to move.

Siren was so close. The tip of the axe cut the side of her face, leaving a nasty cut. Slowly the monster of men stood up, towering over us all. "Now," he boomed, "the real battle begins." He walked forward, the ground shaking with each step.

"Do you remember me, you monster?" Felix roared, stepping out in front of us all.

Chris looked down at the knight. "Ah, you came back. I am glad to have another chance of killing you without your little time bomb protecting you." Chris lay his hand on the crystal where the girls were frozen. But when he did, it cracked slightly. "Hmm, seems like you guys just made it in time. But it will take time for her to break the seal. Which is more than enough time to kill you all."

Felix roared and charged as do the rest of us. Chris roared at the challenge and lifted the crystal Annie is in and hurled it toward us with blinding speed. It smacked into another group of soldiers, turning the crystal from clear into red smear. I quickly got back to my feet and grabbed my blade. Felix charged with all his might, swinging his large blades, sending sparks off the ground and cutting a large gash into his arm. But his momentum brought him too close to him.

Chris quickly grabbed another soldier who was rushing in to attack by the arm, crushing it and slamming his body into Felix's, sending them both flying. We all stared in awe as Felix slammed against the wall, knocking him unconscious. Then Siren rushed at the mad Titan from behind. She slammed her blade, piercing the back knee. The large man fell to one knee, growling as she twisted her blade, momentarily stopping him for the prince rushed in front of him and grabbed his face. The prince roared as magic flowed through his gauntlets, causing my brother to roar madly, steam filling my brother's eyes he lifted his massive arm up and swiped away the prince into a group of men.

Chris turned around, grabbed the female knight, lifted her into the air, her face full of fear as Chris slammed his fist into her. She soared and skipped across the ground. Blood trail smeared across the ground. I ran to her and saw if she was okay, but as I reached her, the black knight started to stand, her body shaking as she forced herself to stand. I had seen and been on the other side of his blows. She looked at me and spit blood to the ground. "What are you looking at?" she growled. She went to reach her blade and stubbled forward, but I caught her as she fell.

My brother turned to me. Our eyes met. "Did you end it quickly, brother? Our sisters slayed by your hands."

"They gave me no choice, brother," I bit out. "You were once my family, but I have to end this now."

The mad Titan tensed as he roared, "Neither did you." His body tensed and in a blur, he flashed toward me. I had barely enough time to shove Siren out of the way as his body slammed into the wall behind us. The ground trembled as he impacted the wall. I rushed forward and stabbed my blade into Chris's back, driving my blade deep.

The monster roared in rage and slowly recovered. But as he did, everyone rushed and drove their blades into the flesh of this monster. He growled but seemed to be having a hard time standing. But then, in a moment, steam poured from his wounds. It's The Titan roars out with fury as blistering heat, there was no chance of us holding on as weapons and all were scattered. I could see nothing but I felt my wreaked body collide with the cold ground beneath me as I came to skidding ha. I came to a stop and breathed deep. My skin was burned and my body was packed with pain. I looked up, my vision blurring in and out.

Another man fell before my brother in a bloody mess. I struggled to one knee when I saw the mad Titan grabbing his axe from the wall. I grasped for air when I looked down to my arm. *Damn, I don't want to risk turning all the way.* I roared in frustration and my arm started to change. The bones snapped and my arm grew.

I bit out in agony as my fingers changed.

"William," someone yelled, "stay with us, damn it."

I struggled with the beast inside wanting full control. It clawed just under the skin, fighting for control. I roared as the change only stayed to my arm. I hated the sight of it: the black skin, the veins bursting red. I looked up to my brother who was grinning. His smile was wide. "Now, brother, I will have the chance to rip it off you like I promised."

"No, now you die." I charged at the mad beast, everyone watching. Chris roared and spun, hurling his mighty axe my way with blinding speed. But I could see it all too clearly. Before the axe hit me, I dodged out of the way and grabbed its handle. The momentum threatened to take me with it, but I roared and hurled the axe back his way with tremendous force.

The Titan's eyes looked wide as the force of the axe threw him into the wall with the axe buried into his chest, and before he could look down in shock, I slammed my fist into his stomach. All I could hear was his groan as I pushed it forward into his gut. I looked up at my brother. "Now die, you bastard," I roared, tears flowing from my eyes.

My brother reached down at me, but as I tried to pull away, my hand was stuck. His hand grabbed my throat and lifted me up, steam flowing from his eyes. "I refuse to die to you, brother." Blood was leaking from the corners of his mouth.

I jerked my hand free, blood pouring out, and slammed my fist into his face, doing enough damage to have him drop me. I smacked the ground and desperately gasped for air. But then I heard a loud crack and the sounds of ice hitting the ground. I looked behind me, and Annie was walking forward, eyes burning hot white, a red crystal hanging around her neck. And Quinn was lying on the ground behind her, blood filling the area around her. I tried to get to her but I couldn't.

I noticed my brother starting to recover and started to pull at his axe that had him pinned to the wall. Steam poured around the blade, and I started to crawl backward. Annie walked past me, aura surrounding her. The mad Titan roared at her, but she kept moving forward until she stood before him. He roared at her and reached out to her, but he was just out of reach. "You can't kill me, witch," he growled. "I will get free."

She looked at him and rushed toward, dodging his grasp and touched the hilt of the axe. All I could hear was her whisper. "I know we can't kill you. But this will be your tomb." The crystal glowed bright, and my brother roared. I saw the axe turning into stone as it started to cover his body until he was completely petrified into stone. The survivors all watched in awe of the moment.

My arms returned to normal, causing me pain for the last time, the beast inside lying to rest once more. The white aura faded away, and she started to fall. Felix ran to her and grabbed her before she could fall to the ground.

"Hey, big guy," she said, reaching up to him, "what took you so long?"

"Hey, toothpick," he said while smiling. "I got caught up with your uncle."

She laughed and looked up to the ceiling. "What did you do to him?" Nikolia said, walking forward with Siren who needed help walking. "Is he dead?" he asked, pointing his blade toward the stone-covered man.

"No, he is very much alive. He's just sealed away," she said, breathing deeply. "Only thing I could think of that could stop him. But I couldn't do it without this crystal."

I sighed in relief and rushed to Quinn. She looked up to me. She was gravely wounded and burned. Annie came.

"Help me," I pleaded. She rushed over, held out her hand.

"Please don't go, Quinn," I pleaded. Our eyes locked.

But she smiled with blood coming out from her mouth. "I told you I would see you again."

I leaned down and kissed her as a burst of light consumed the three of us. The world blurred out, then in a flash, I was standing in front of a huge city with towering white wall. A castle that is majestic burst into flames, pouring from the windows. I turned to see a city ablaze. Then in a flash, I saw men and women and children falling before me, then I saw a familiar face: Annie in a white dress, holding her hands up and screaming before blood flowed over her face, but she looked different in the face. The despair of this vision raked my body with grief. Was that me or just a vision of what's to come.

But as soon as it came, it was gone. My vision came too, and Annie's body was glowing bright but soon fell. She didn't look herself but someone between Annie and Quinn and a red crystal was embedded into her chest. I tried to reach my arm up to her, but she swung her hand, blasting me feet away. "Annie." I reached out, trying to explain something I myself couldn't even explain.

Felix jumped in between us and looked at her. "Is that still you?"

Her eyes were pale white. "We must go. I have no time to explain." Well as the rest of the surviving members formed a circle around her, "What is happening? I am confused on what I saw."

"It wasn't me I swear."

"What did you see?" the prince bit out to his wife.

"I am sorry, William," she said, "but I can't lie." Tears were rolling down one of her eyes. "He'll kill us all."

The words shattered my world into a thousand small pieces. "No, I wouldn't."

Felix looked back at the small woman. "Are you sure?"

She wiped the tears from her face and nodded.

Felix's head dropped. his head raises and his eyes looked sad. "I told you I saw you as a brother and would gladly fight by your side. But you have become a threat which I cannot ignore. You shall share this tomb with your family, but your name shall not be forgotten. We will tell stories of what you did here today."

The words brought no comfort as everything was for nothing. Then I saw Annie stood up. Nikolia approached his wife and grinned. His eyes met mine. "You are no longer needed, William. You can live the rest of your life in this tomb."

My sadness threatened to take over. I stood up to see the prince grinning at me. I grabbed my hair as my mind started to fracture. "You would kill me after everything we have been through," I roared. "No."

My body shook in anger. The ground shook violently, and the ceiling seemed to be caving in. Rocks fell around me as I tried to dodge them. But then I noticed Annie looking and chanting magic around them. The surviving members became shrouded in black smoke. I reached out to them. "No, you bastards, don't leave me."

I rushed to them and leaped through the air. But in a moment, they were gone. Darkness began to shroud me as rocks fell to pieces, one striking me in the head. I looked up and could see the moon somehow. Maybe it's my imagination. I reached my hand up, trying to grasp for my salvation, and roared as blackness overtook me. The hall hadn't entirely collapsed, but I was gravely wounded, crawling to the stairway. "Damn it all." I looked up to see the staircase blocked off, but not by rubble, but some black mist. I crawled over rubble and corpses. I reached out to touch it, but it burned my hand. I didn't have much time to think before my vision faded away. What a sad way to go.

CPSIA information can be obtained
at www.ICGtesting.com
Printed in the USA
BVHW032026181120
593515BV00002BA/205

9 781098 054762